# Never Let Her Go

## Books by Jane Tesh

### The Grace Street Mysteries

*Stolen Hearts*

*Mixed Signals*

*Now you See It*

*Just You Wait*

*Baby, Take a Bow*

*Death by Dragonfly*

*Gone Daddy Blues*

*Fatal Fantasy*

*Deadly Dreams*

### The Madeline Maclin Mysteries

*A Case of Imagination*

*A Hard Bargain*

*A Little Learning*

*A Bad Reputation*

*Evil Turns*

*A Wild Ride*

*Buried Secrets*

### Stand Alone Mysteries

*Ghost Light*

# Never Let Her Go

## Grace Street Mystery #10

### Jane Tesh

Savvy Press

Library of Congress Control Number:

ISBN: 9781939113757   Trade Paperback
ISBN: 9781939113764   Kindle

Savvy Press
481 Beattie Hollow Rd
Salem NY 12865
www.savvypress.com
info@savvypress.com

Cover design: **François Thisdale**

Printed in the United States of America

*To all my friends at the Mount Airy Public Library.*

*Thanks for your continuing support!*

# CHAPTER ONE

*"Dancing Queen"*

After a couple of months of calm at 302 Grace Street, and just when I thought everything was settled, here came another crisis.

This past May, we'd weathered the birth of Camden's daughter Elise, mainly because, thanks to his psychic ability and hers, he could communicate with the baby. I could too, so I was in on all the drama—Ellin stoically refusing to scream, Elise calling out, *I'm on my way! Ooo, there's a turn. Daddy, can you see my head yet? Is Dave there?* and other things her not-psychic mother couldn't hear, which was all for the best.

Dave wasn't there. I was in the waiting room with Kary, who kept asking for the play-by-play report and laughing at my expressions. When we finally got to see the baby, she was snuggled in her mother's arms asleep, a perfect little girl with wisps of blond hair. Camden sat by the bed, his hand resting gently on the baby's back, his eyes shining.

I didn't have to have a link with him to know exactly how he felt. I remembered the first time I'd held my Lindsey. It had taken a long time to come to terms with her death, but now I saw her and heard her encouraging little spirit. She would always be eight years old and look as she did in her second-grade school picture, long brown curls, dark brown eyes like mine, and the same sweet smile I thought I had lost. Lindsey often helped me on my cases, but recently, she'd warned me about evil spirits on the loose. Camden and I had encountered one of these—or thought we did—but things had been calm.

Until today.

This steamy Friday morning in July, Kary had left at nine for an interview for a teaching job at Ivan Elementary in Mooresville. Ordinarily, we'd both be happy about a job offer, but Mooresville was an hour away from Parkland, an hour and a half away from the charmed circle of 302 Grace Street. Her faithful Ford Fiesta, Turbo, was okay for driving around town, but a commute to Mooresville every day would require a new car, which she couldn't afford. I also couldn't afford it, and probably Kary wouldn't have accepted it even if I could. It was entirely possible that she would have to move, and if she moved, then I'd have to go with her.

Move away from Elise, my psychic godchild? Move away when mysterious evil forces might return? But I had to be with Kary. This was going to be one hell of a choice.

So I was sitting in my office feeling glum and listening to a particularly relevant jazz song called "Home No More" when my cell phone rang. I was hoping for a client, but it was my friend Jordan Finley of the Parkland Police Department. Maybe he needed my help to solve yet another mystery that baffled the force.

"Another serial killer bothering you, Finley?"

"I wish," he said. "You ever hear of a singer named Sherry White?"

"Sherry White? Yes, I've heard of her." It was hard not to hear of her. People fell down in crying fits when she sang. They went to her movies over and over, and whenever she had a concert, tickets sold out in minutes.

"I need a few extra guys to help with security at the Parkland Auditorium tonight and next Saturday," Jordan said.

A job was a job. "Sure."

"Meet me around seven at the back door."

"What's the deal with Miss White?" I asked.

"You'll see when you get here."

"All right," I said. "Thanks."

I needed the distraction—and here was another one at the front door.

All of Camden's friends just barge in, but this person knocked, so I figured it was someone looking for me and the Randall Detective Agency.

A tall woman stood outside the screen door. She wore an expensive-looking black suit jacket and skirt with a black and gold scarf fastened over one shoulder by a gold brooch.

"Hello," I said. "May I help you?"

"Well, hello," she said in a husky voice. At least at first glance, I thought *she*—shoulder-length brown hair and carefully plucked brows. But then I noticed the Adam's apple and the size fifteen feet in huge shiny black high heels. "My, aren't you the handsome one. Is this Cam's house?"

Camden came up behind me holding little Elise, and when the man saw him, he shrieked. "Cam! My God, you look wonderful! Is this your baby girl? I can't believe it!" He angled around me and then Elise to give Camden a hug. "You haven't aged a second, you wretched boy. What's your secret?"

"Brown sugar Pop-Tarts," Camden said, grinning.

"Oh, my lord, are you still eating those things?"

"It's great to see you, Denny," he said. "What brings you to town?"

"Why, the show, of course."

"The show?"

"*South Pacific.* Didn't you know? Parkland's Little Theater director is a dear dear friend. The show goes up in two weeks, he's had all sorts of actors drop out, and he pleaded with me to come help. I thought I'd bunk with you, if it's not too much trouble."

"No trouble at all."

"You must do the show, too! You could be my baby boy, just like old times." He eyed me up and down. "Are you going to introduce me?"

"David Randall, Denny Kowalski."

Denny extended a long-fingered hand. The nails were bright red. "A pleasure."

I shook hands. "Nice to meet you."

"Now, let me get my things," he said. "This is so exciting!"

"Baby boy?" I said as Denny pranced down the walk to his yellow Le Baron.

"When I was sick in San Francisco, Denny took me in," Camden said. "One of the nicest guys you'll ever meet."

"Did he deck you out in a little pinafore to see how cute you'd look?"

"He wanted to, but he understood I wasn't interested. It was like having a big sister. A really big sister. Hold Elise for a second, and I'll help him with his things."

Even at two months old, Elise leaned toward me as if she knew I'd take her, and of course I did. "Your mother's going to love this," I told her as Camden helped Denny wrangle his color-coordinated luggage out of the car.

Once Denny's two suitcases and three garment bags had been hauled inside, Denny continued to admire Elise. "Now how old is this baby doll?"

"Two months old," Camden said.

"She's gorgeous. She looks just like you, the same big blue eyes, the same blond hair. It's even a mess like yours. Hello, sweetheart. Give Auntie Denny a kiss."

Elise gave him a long unblinking stare and then made a chuckling noise as if catching some secret joke.

"What a doll. What a heartbreaker," Denny said. "Are you a mind-reader, too, baby doll?"

"Yes, she is," Camden said.

"Dearie me, what a time you'll have."

"She's the first of three."

Denny's plucked eyebrows went up in mock horror. "What? Are you populating the world with blond psychic babies? Your own personal Village of the Damned?"

Elise chuckled again.

"I think she understands me!" Denny said, delighted.

"She has a very good sense of humor," Camden said.

"Not like her mom," I said.

"Yes, of course, you're married." Denny looked around. "When do I get to meet the lucky woman?"

"She'll be home after five," he said. "She produces programs for the Psychic Service Network."

"A whole family of psychics! I feel so déclassé."

"Ellie's not psychic," Camden said, "and she's sensitive about it."

Denny made a locking motion at his lips. "You know me, the soul of discretion. So tell me, what have you been doing with yourself since your traveling days?"

Camden had left his foster home at age sixteen and wandered the country, doing odd jobs and learning to cope with his talent. I'd heard most of this, so I handed Elise back over, excused myself, and went into my office, hoping I could make the phone ring with a rich client on the other end of the line. But I could hear them laughing in the island, our sitting area of well-worn furniture, which included my seat of choice, a blue armchair, the green corduroy couch where Camden liked to lounge, Kary's little rocking chair with its red velvet cushion, a coffee table overflowing with magazines, clipped coupons, and books, and a worn but colorful carpet with tattered fringe. Ellin had attempted to make things match by adding some nice lamps and cushions, but the island was still a fine example of Bohemian Castaway.

"You did what?" I heard Denny say. "Oh, that's hilarious. That is too funny."

After a while, he appeared at my door. "So this is where the famous detective solves all those dastardly crimes."

"You bet. All the crimes all the time."

"Ah, yes." He sauntered in. "Cam's fixing Elise another bottle." He lifted the edge of the curtains, sniffed, and continued to inspect the room. The desk and bookshelf met with his approval. "Very homey. Medium-boiled, I'd say."

"Say what you like. It's all mine."

He spied the framed picture of Lindsey on the bookshelf. "Is this your little girl? She's precious."

"Thank you."

"Does she live here, too?"

"She's with her grandparents." A safe enough answer. Lindsey's mother's folks had passed away, so it was possible she ran into them on the Other Side.

Fortunately, Denny didn't ask any more questions about her. He sat down in the chair I have for clients, crossed his long legs, and readjusted the hem of his skirt. "Are you on a case right now?"

"Nope. Just helping out with security for Sherry White's concerts."

"Sherry White? Oh, my lord! I used to do a spot-on impersonation of her in my show. One of my best, if I do say so myself. Poor thing! She's in somewhat of a downward slide these days."

"Why is that?"

He shrugged. "The competition among female singers is extremely tough. Plus there are so many up and coming young divas. I imagine Sherry's having a rough go of it."

"She's still popular, though, isn't she?"

"Oh, she has a rabid fan base. But I did notice there would be less and less call for her in my show. Liza Minnelli and Cher, now, they never go out of style. They love them over at the Pyramid. That's where I'll be performing when I'm not at the theater, so don't you worry. I won't be in your way."

"No problem," I said. "Any big sister of Camden's is a sister of mine."

He laughed. "Is that what he called me? How appropriate. Did he tell you how we met?"

"Not in detail."

Denny combed his red nails through his hair. "I found him in the alley behind my building, absolutely full of fever, poor thing. He was sick for days, but he kept waking up saying, 'Justin. Don't trust Justin.' Well, Paul Justin happened to be the man wanting my act for his new club, and I was this close to signing a contract. I did some digging, and damned if the man wasn't involved in this huge drug cartel, and my ass would have been grass if I'd been associated in any way with his club. I mean, my career would have been over. When Cam got better, he told me all kinds of stuff about my future and who to sign with. I was so excited because in San Francisco, we are rolling in magic, honey, all sorts of New Age wonders, you name it, and to have my very own psychic was thrilling. And he was so darling. I did so want to put him in the act, but he didn't care to dress up. Such a pity."

I hadn't heard this story before. "When was this?"

"Let's see. Oh, several years ago. Ten? Fifteen? I swear he looks exactly the same. Has he made some pact with the devil lately?"

"Not lately."

"My, my. I was tripping down memory lane there, wasn't I?" He didn't say anything for a long moment. "This is going to sound a little crazy, but I feel I should tell you the real reason I came to Parkland." Again he hesitated. "It's personal."

"You don't have to tell me anything."

"I know, but since I'll be staying here for a while, I should explain."

"If you want to."

He took another long pause. Then he clasped his hands in his lap. "I didn't just come all the way to Parkland to star in a show. I'm looking for my soul mate. I thought that Yvette, my ex-partner, was the one, but it didn't work out."

Not what I expected. "Sorry to hear that."

Denny sighed and suddenly looked like a tired man in women's clothing. "I trusted Yvette. I thought we had something special. We were the dearest of friends. We knew each other's innermost secrets. We called ourselves the Divine Divas. Our act consisted of impersonating famous singers like Cher and Liza, of course, and Tina Turner and Barbara Streisand. We'd worked our way through the seedier nightclubs to become headliners for one of the best drag clubs in San Francisco. Along the way, there had been all the petty jealousies, rivalries, romances, and screaming fits associated with a team, but we finally made enough money to feel secure and had our own loft overlooking Castro Street. That's when Yvette became restless.

"She kept saying, 'We have to do more, we have to expand the act.' Well, heavenly days, I thought we were doing great. If we added to the act, we'd need Lord knows how many more wigs and shoes, and let me tell you, those don't come cheap." Denny stuck out his large high-heeled foot. "I've never been easy to fit. These cost me five hundred and sixty-two dollars and fifty-nine cents. Yvette wanted to do Madonna and Gloria Estavan and Celine Dion. I said, 'Vette, you don't have to be every woman in the world.' But she loved showing off. Then one day I came home, and she was gone. Didn't even leave me a note." He sighed. "I know Cam has found the love of his life. Dare I ask if you've found yours?"

"Yes," I said. "But there were two wives before her and a few bumps in the road. If you don't mind me asking, what exactly makes you think your soul mate is in Parkland?"

"Well, if she wasn't in San Francisco, where on earth would she be? I thought Cam might know."

"Did Camden see anything for you?"

"Well, he tried, but he said my vibes are too agitated for him to get a clear picture." He gave me a sad little smile. "Thanks for listening, David. I'm just going to have to let Yvette go. I know finding soul mates isn't in your job description. That's something that just has to happen. But I appreciate you letting me ramble on."

"No problem," I said.

Denny turned as Camden came in, Elise tucked in one arm gulping from her bottle as if it were her last.

"Cam, you have the most wonderful friends!"

Camden gave me a grateful look. "I told you he'd understand."

"And I appreciate it so much," Denny said. "Well, I'd better get my things unpacked. But if there's anything else you need to know about Sherry White, David, you just ask me."

I hoped I wouldn't have to know anything else about Sherry White, but I thanked him. A chugging noise announced Kary's Turbo coming down Grace Street. The little neon green car turned into the driveway, parked beside my white '67 Plymouth Fury, and Kary got out.

I met her as she came up the walk, smiling, her long blond hair smoothed back in an elegant ponytail. She had on a light blue dress in some soft silky material that smoothed over her slim hips and flared around her long legs.

"How'd it go?" I asked.

"Let's sit down." We took seats in the porch rocking chairs. Kary gave me a serious look with her warm brown eyes. "The job's mine if I want it."

My heart sank. "Do you want it?"

She sighed. "You know how hard I've looked for a job in Parkland. There's nothing available right now, and I can't afford to wait until there is. Ivan Elementary is a beautiful school, and the opening is for a second grade teacher, which is my favorite grade. The school has all the latest technology: computers in every classroom, smart boards, closed-circuit TV."

"What about your guidance counselor degree?" I asked. Kary had been working toward achieving this goal for some time.

"I can transfer my credits to Mooresville Community College and continue classes there, if only—" her voice faltered. "If only I could move 302 Grace Street to Mooresville."

"We'll find our own Grace Street."

As she looked around the porch, I knew what she was thinking. It wouldn't be the same. Maybe we could find a house like this with a big front porch, rocking chairs, a porch swing, and huge oak trees to keep us cool during the summer months. Maybe we could find a home with a welcoming atmosphere, a living room with a faded blue arm chair and a green corduroy sofa, and two cats that played with the carpet fringe. But Camden's house had been Kary's home and her refuge for a long time, probably the only real home she'd ever had. As for me, how could I not love the place where I met Kary?

"We'll make it work," I said. "You'll have your piano. You'll have your old white robe to wear in the mornings, and I'll have your Diet Coke ready every afternoon when you come home. I might even find a church somewhere so I can sit beside you and share a hymnbook."

I'd hoped to make her smile, but she was too concerned. "What about your agency? You've worked so hard to get it going. If we move to Mooresville, you'll have to start over."

"I'll open a branch office there."

Still no smile. Kary twisted the silver heart-shaped ring she wore on her right hand. I'd given her that ring one Christmas. A friendship ring, I'd said. It was as close to an engagement ring as I was likely to get. "I wish Mooresville weren't so far away. I wouldn't mind a thirty-minute commute. Turbo could handle that.

But an hour and a half is too much."

"Don't give up yet," I said. "We may be able to find a solution."

We sat in awkward silence for a while. Then she went inside to break the news to Camden. I stared at the oak trees, still fresh and green, the sun still shining, the birds still chirping.

Damn it. After Kary's announcement, I expected the world to tilt and heave, but life went on.

# CHAPTER TWO

### *"Dance of the Demon"*

The only thing that brightened my day was waiting for Ellin to get home at five from her job at the Psychic Service Network and meet our latest house guest. Our most recent tenants, Harley and Farley Fiddler, had made enough money from weightlifting competitions and their jobs at Kendall Furniture to move into an apartment closer to the gym downtown. Our remaining tenant, Stuart King, who lived across from me at the back of the second floor, was off visiting relatives. Kary and I shared my bedroom, but she kept a room for herself at the front. That left two middle rooms and another front room. Denny chose the latter and made happy noises about the charming view of the trees and flowers. He was delighted to meet Kary and extremely interested to hear about her pageant queen experiences. Once he was settled in, he and Kary sat in the island and exchanged fashion tips (including a raid on Denny's wardrobe) while Camden played with Elise on the sofa. By the time Ellin arrived, Denny was a vision in a silky red kimono and feathered slippers, his hair tied with a matching red ribbon, his long face beaming with a faint five o'clock shadow.

"This must be the little woman! Isn't she gorgeous! Hello, you lucky thing."

Ellin did look gorgeous in navy blue slacks and a light blue silk blouse that covered her post-baby waist and made her blonde curls a rich shade of gold. Her crescent moon earrings matched the pin on her lapel. She'd actually agreed to stay home the first two weeks after Elise was born, never admitting she needed to rest and commanding the troops at the Psychic Service Network from her laptop, but now she was back at the studio full time. She looked up at Denny who came forward, one hand extended.

"You must be a friend of Cam's," she said.

Her tone was polite, but she shot a dangerous look in Camden's direction.

"One of his oldest and dearest," Denny said. "Denny Kowalski, at your service. I can't tell you how grateful I am for the room. I promise I'll be quiet as a little mouse. You'll never know I'm here." Before Ellin could say anything else, Denny gave a little scream and turned to Camden. "Wait a minute! This is the girl, the girl you talked about."

"Yes, she's the one," Camden said.

Ellin looked puzzled. Denny explained. "You see, dearie, everyone was so taken with Cam, but he kept saying no to all offers. No, he'd say, there's a girl in North Carolina. Did I believe this fairy tale?"

She glanced at Camden. "When was this?"

"Before I came to Parkland," he said.

She thought about it and smiled. "Years before we met?"

"I knew you were here somewhere."

Denny beamed at them. "He'd say there's a girl in North Carolina. She's the one. Over and over. Of course, I had no idea what he meant, but he was so certain, I told all his admirers he was spoken for. Now I see it was true all along. I should have known."

Ellin gave Camden a kiss. The baby leaned for her, so she took Elise and gave her a kiss, too. "Well, if I'm the one, Cam, then maybe you'll do something for me."

"Uh, oh," he said.

Despite his continued protests, Ellin had insisted that Camden remain a part of the Psychic Service. "We lost one of our sponsors today," she said. "Candle De-Lite. The owner's retiring, and his son doesn't want the business."

"I'm not sure I can get another sponsor for you," he said.

"Leave that part to me. I want to make sure our remaining sponsors are happy, and they would be happy if you paid them a little visit."

"Why meeting me should make a difference, I don't know, but I'll do it." He hesitated. "I don't have to tell anyone's fortune, or anything?"

"It would be wonderful if you would," she said.

"Ellie, you know I try not to get involved with that kind of thing anymore."

"Unless Randall asks you."

My cell phone rang, cutting short the beginning of a major quarrel. Camden and Elise both got The Look. "It's Jordan, for you," Camden said to me.

Ellin sighed, exasperated. "If you'd just come do something like that for the show."

"Slight change of plans," Jordan said when I answered. "When you get here, come on into the auditorium, and can you come a little earlier than seven, say, six-thirty?"

"No problem." I ended the call and said to Camden, "It's my turn to cook dinner, but Jordan needs me at six-thirty for this Sherry White thing. Can I switch with you?"

Both Ellin and Kary gasped. Ellin's eyes widened. Her hands went out as if she meant to clutch my arm. The fact she might consider touching me signaled something drastic.

"What was that about Sherry White?" she asked.

"Jordan's a little short-handed and asked if I'd help with security for her concerts," I said.

"Oh, my God, I hope you said yes."

"I did."

"You have got to get me a ticket."

"Me, too," Kary said. "David, if there's any way. . ."

"She is my absolute favorite," Ellin said. "She's unbelievable."

"I don't think I'm familiar with her work," I said, just to be annoying.

Ellin rolled her eyes. "She's had six songs go to number one. I know you've heard 'Angel of Love.'"

I'd heard it, all right. You couldn't escape it. A sappy, lovesick tune, tailor-made for elevators. I prefer something with more life and punch, say, the New Black Eagle Jazz Band's rendition of anything.

"It's pretty goopy," I said.

"Goopy? What kind of word is that? It's a beautiful song."

"Okay, maybe it's a beautiful song, but I'll never understand why people worship celebrities. They're just human beings doing a job."

"I don't care what you think about Sherry White or her music, if you can get me a ticket, I might overlook a certain problem you've been having with the rent," Ellin said.

"Blackmail," I said. "I won't stand for it."

"In case you've forgotten, Kary's a fan, too," she said.

I knew then I was crawling through broken glass to get tickets. "I'll do my best."

"Dearie, I could do Sherry White in concert," Denny said to Ellin. "I'm a little out of practice, but I know all her songs."

"Did you see her in *One For Sorrow*?" Kary asked. "I think that's her best movie."

"Oh, you can't beat *Days of Splendor*," he said.

"I love that one," Ellin said. "But I really think she did her best work in *The Shepherd's Daughter*."

"Oh, my lord! Her hair in that one is to die for!"

It sounded as if this could go on all night.

"I'll fix dinner," Camden said.

Elise leaned back toward him, so he took the baby. Ellin joined Kary and Denny in the island where they continued their discussion of Sherry White's movies. I followed Camden into the kitchen. For once, I wanted to know the future. "Will Kary and I have to move?"

He put Elise in her little carrier on the counter. "I hope not."

"Can't you check ahead and see if there's a teaching position in Parkland for her?"

His eyes had lost some of their bright blue color. He'd taken Kary in when her parents rejected her for becoming pregnant, not even relenting when she lost the baby and her ability to have children. If she moved, he'd lose a member of his constructed family, a sister, someone who knew what it was like to be an outcast. "So far, I haven't seen anything. I wish I could. Another fine example of my useless talent."

Camden's considerable psychic ability was often unpredictable, but he was always right. I sat down at the counter beside Elise. The baby reached over to catch one of my fingers and attempted to pull it into her mouth. I tugged my finger back, and she pulled it forward as if she'd invented a new game. "This might be the break you've been looking for," I said. "If I'm not in the house, Ellin's going to be very happy. She might stop pestering you to move."

Because of the constant turnover of peculiar tenants and because I lived here, Ellin wanted to move to a new house in a more upscale neighborhood, but 302 Grace had been Camden's home since he'd come to Parkland, and he often mentioned the spirit of the former owner was happy he was taking care of her house.

"I can deal with that a lot easier than having everyone gone," he said.

A sudden thought gave me a chill. Lindsey's little spirit often relied on Camden to get her messages through. "Would Lindsey be able to reach me if I'm not here?"

"That's a good question," he said. "I don't know. You need to ask her."

That was something I'd definitely have to find out before I left 302 Grace and Parkland.

***

I arrived at the Parkland Auditorium a little before six-thirty and got my first close up view of Sherry White. I'd seen plenty of pictures of her. She was tall and thin with small close-set brown eyes and a mane of orangey curls. I wasn't a fan of her singing style. All her songs began with a whisper and ended with a sonic boom as Sherry strained to reach a high note somewhere beyond human hearing. I'd actually seen *The Shepherd's Daughter*, a mushy costume epic, because Kary wanted to see it. In the movie, Sherry White had fifty different outfits and ten indistinguishable songs and somehow managed to snare a handsome farmer who just happened to be a prince in disguise.

Maybe she was dynamic and appealing in person.

Nope.

Her Highness was throwing an on-stage fit because someone forgot to take out the yellow M&Ms from the candy dish and yellow was her unlucky color. She then complained about the size of her dressing room, the lack of a proper chair, and the fact that one of the light bulbs surrounding the makeup mirror had burned out. Then she had another tantrum with a lighting technician until he readjusted one tiny light to get the right sparkle in her hair.

I met Jordan Finley at the front of the stage where he was giving orders to three uniformed police officers. "Thanks so much," I said.

He grinned. "Don't disturb the serious artiste." He introduced me to the others. "Everyone, this is David Randall. He'll be helping with backstage security."

I shook hands with the other officers. "I thought stars of Miss White's magnitude traveled with a pack of security."

"She's managed to alienate most of the security teams in the business," Jordan said.

"How did the Parkland PD get the gig?"

He shrugged a large shoulder. "The owner of the auditorium's a good friend, and Sherry White, Incorporated, made a sizable donation to our Christmas fund."

Another screech from Miss White made us turn.

"I cannot believe this stupid auditorium doesn't have enough blue follow spots! Get me some right now!"

Her hapless assistant cringed. "Miss White, I'm sure we brought enough."

She glared at him. "I said get me some more! And I want my sable wrap. It's freezing in here."

The assistant hurried off and another ran up with the fur coat she wanted. Jordan's crooked eyebrow told me exactly what he thought of such histrionics.

"Would you believe someone's threatened to kill her?"

"That sweet helpless flower? What's the world coming to?"

Sherry White pointed a long orange fingernail at us. "Why are you all standing around? Don't you have jobs?"

"Jordan Finley, Parkland Police Department," Jordan said. "I'll have four officers on duty at all times, Miss White."

"Four? Is that all?"

"Yes, ma'am, as well as Mr. Randall here."

Sherry White was not impressed. "You do understand my life has been threatened?"

"Yes, ma'am. I believe you said you had several personal bodyguards."

"I certainly do," she said, as if daring him to challenge her.

Looking around the auditorium, I saw no evidence of bodyguards, but I didn't say anything. Jordan tried to be tactful.

"That should be enough."

"Enough" was not in Miss White's vocabulary. "It most certainly is not. I told you I wanted every available man you have."

"Every available man is here, Miss White. We're in the middle of several important cases, and this is all I can spare."

She stewed a while and then said, "I'll discuss this with your superiors later." Then she shrieked for the lights and went back to her rehearsal.

"Your superiors," I said. "That would be you. What's this about death threats?"

"Letters. Standard stuff. 'Don't perform tonight, or you'll wish you hadn't.' 'This is your last concert.' 'Sing and die.'"

"Any suspects?"

"From the looks of things, I'd say everybody she comes in contact with," he said. "I want you to stay backstage and keep an eye out for anyone suspicious. We'll be checking the audience as they come in, metal detectors, the usual." He took a green plastic badge out of his pocket. "This is yours. Anybody who's backstage should be wearing one."

I thanked him for backstage duty and he grinned again.

"You won't be able to hear her as well back there."

"So what's the deal with these concerts?" I asked.

"This one tonight's for her regular fans who follow her everywhere. Tomorrow she's giving a special one for the Wishing Star Foundation, a big charity event. Then she's doing the regular concert next Saturday."

"She's hanging around Parkland a week? How'd we get so lucky?"

"She says she needs the time to meditate." He spoke to the other officers. "Briggs, I want you and March to take the opposite sides of the stage. Stanley, you're with me."

I went backstage to check things out. There were dressing rooms for the band and the backup singers and a larger, fancier room for Sherry White. A short flight of steps led up to the stage. The exit was down a short well-lit hallway. Coming up the hallway was a young woman all in black: tight black jeans, black turtleneck sweater, black leather jacket, black shoulder bag, black shoes. With her long straight dark hair and bright blue eyes smudged with dark liner, she looked like the leader of an all-girl rock band, but when she smiled and spoke, the tough-gal image dissolved. Then she looked more like a kid trying out her older sister's cool clothes.

"Hi! I'm Valerie Banner. I write the 'New Faces' column for the *Parkland Herald*. I'm doing a series of articles on Sherry White. You must be one of her agents."

"How do you figure that?" I asked.

"You're dressed too nicely to be a roadie, and the band's all in blue."

I noticed she had a green badge like mine, so I figured she was legit. "My name's David Randall. I'm helping with security."

She dug in her shoulder bag and brought out her phone. She pushed a few buttons to record our conversation. "What's the scoop on that? I hear she's been getting some threatening letters."

"That's what I'm hoping to find out."

"So, what do you think of Sherry? Be honest, now. This article's going to be gritty."

I doubted if Ms. Banner had ever been close to gritty. Close up, the blue eyes beamed with innocence. "I've just met her," I said. "She seems to be your typical temperamental artist."

"What do you think of her music?"

I was saved by a knock on the exit door. "Excuse me." I went to check and found a man standing just outside, smoking a cigarette, a tall thin man with a sharp beak of a nose.

Tony Kenner. Great.

Kenner was a slick, self-important weasel who thought he was God's gift to the newspaper world, even though he worked for the *Galaxy News Weekly*, Parkland's skuzziest tabloid, a lurid little paper that specialized in aliens, ghosts, mutant animals, and JFK and Elvis sightings. He was the kind of guy who's always smiling as if he knows the answer to everything and he's not going to tell you.

"What the hell are you doing here?" I asked him.

He grinned his weasel grin. "Same question back at you."

"I'm one of Miss White's bodyguards."

"I got an interview with Miss White."

"I doubt that," I said. "Besides, have you observed her in action? She'll chop you up."

He shrugged. "Comes with the job."

"Got a backstage pass?"

He patted his clothes and gave me another grin. "Gee, I must have left it in my other jacket."

"Well, you're not going to bother her today," I said. "Unless you think you can get past me."

He eyed me. We'd had a few altercations before. "I really got an interview."

"I really want you to get lost. This is an exit. Use it."

I pushed him out the door and made sure it slammed shut. When I turned around, I was eye to eye with Miss White.

"What was all that about?" she asked.

"Tony Kenner, a reporter from Parkland's premiere tabloid, the *Galaxy News Weekly*. He said he had an interview with you."

"He certainly does not."

"I didn't think so."

Her gaze was reassessing. "At least *you* seem to know what you're doing. Now I must find Diamond."

"You've lost some jewelry?"

"No, no. Diamond is my psychic advisor. I don't make a move without consulting her. Where is she?"

"What does she look like?" I asked.

"You'd know her instantly. She has an otherworldly air that's unmistakable. Diamond! My God, where is that woman?" She glared at Valerie Banner, who'd been watching avidly. "Are you still here?"

"I was hoping for a few more words, Miss White."

"You'll have to wait. In case you haven't noticed, there's a crisis here." As she swept off toward her dressing room, an assistant approached, trembling.

"Miss White, Diamond's gone."

Sherry paused in mid-stride. "Gone? What do you mean?"

"She left this morning. She said she couldn't—"

The assistant faltered, but I knew what he meant. Diamond couldn't take it anymore.

Sherry White's famous four octave range made a great shriek. "*What?* Are you telling me that ungrateful little wretch *left* me? Right before a major concert? Is she *insane?* She knows I can't function without her! Find her! Bring her back!"

Sherry White then did something I've never seen anyone do. She flung herself back into her dressing room and tore it apart. Valerie stared in amazement, and I stood back and watched as Sherry shredded pillows, threw lamps to the floor, yanked pictures off their hooks, kicked over chairs, and tossed the bowls of M&Ms against the wall.

Valerie held her phone steady, recording the carnage, until Sherry noticed what she was doing. She snatched the phone out of Valerie's hand.

"How dare you, you little nobody! I didn't give you permission to video me!" She stabbed at the phone to stop the recording and then threw it on the floor.

Valerie gasped and grabbed it up, narrowly avoiding the next round of thrown objects.

When Sherry had finished destroying everything that could be destroyed, she plopped down on the remaining chair, breathing hard.

"Good work," I said. "That solved your problem."

Her gaze was murderous, but, hey, I live with the Queen of Murderous Stares. "Get out."

"Is this what fame does to people, turns them into sulky two-year olds?"

"How dare you speak to me like that? Get out!"

I couldn't believe it, but there was a sob in her voice. "I thought I'd hang around for the next show."

"You don't know anything about this." She wiped away tears. "Without Diamond, I can't do the concert. I have to know how it will go."

Okay, this train was heading off the rails. "You do hundreds of concerts a year. Are you telling me you can't go on until Diamond says it's okay?"

She tossed her orange mop of hair. "I know it sounds ridiculous to someone like you. You probably don't believe in anything. But I have to know before I go out there. The pressure's amazingly intense. I have to be perfect for my fans. I have to know I'll be perfect."

"Your fans don't care," I said. "They're nuts about you."

"Shut up! You don't know."

I'd spent a previous case surrounded by emotionally stunted actors. I recognized the signs. "You have stage fright."

Her little eyes went as wide as they could. "Don't you dare say that!"

"It's not a crime. Obviously you can get over it and perform."

She hugged herself. "You have no idea. It paralyzes me. I have to know the concert will go well. I have to have Diamond! *You* find her! Find her now!"

"What if I bring you someone else?"

That put a pause in her tirade. "That's impossible," she said, but she couldn't keep a hopeful gleam from her little eyes.

"My friend Camden is psychic."

"He couldn't possibly be as good as Diamond."

"I don't think I can find Diamond right away, but I know where Camden is."

She hesitated only a moment. "He'd better be good."

"Give me twenty minutes."

Valerie Banner trailed me up the hall. "You have a psychic friend? This is terrific! This is just the kind of thing our readers will gobble up."

I stopped so suddenly, she almost ran into me. "If you're going to be a problem, I can have you removed, just like Kenner."

She smiled. "You wouldn't do that. I'm local color girl, that's all."

"I'm sure that even with a busted phone, you've got enough material to write about Sherry's big blow up and her missing Diamond."

"Well, sure."

"Just keep out of the way."

"Okay, okay," she said. "But a psychic friend! That's just so neat."

# CHAPTER THREE

## *"She's Always Dancing"*

I don't know what Sherry expected, but it wasn't a small blond man in jeans and a blue shirt with the sleeves rolled up, his sneakers untied and his hair in his eyes. We all stood in the dressing room while I made the introductions. When Camden smiled at Sherry, I saw her expression change, a faint pink coloring her cheeks. Suddenly, she was all charm. She held out her hand.

"Mr. Camden."

"Miss White."

"Sherry, please," she said. "You can't be the psychic."

He was still holding her hand. "Your real name is Edna."

Her cocky grin faded and she jerked her hand away. "No one knows that!" She glared at me. "If you ever tell anyone, I'll kill you."

I held up both hands. "Your secret is safe with me."

Sherry turned back to Camden, her manner completely changed. "How will the concert go? Tell me."

"Very well. Don't worry."

"You're sure? You're absolutely sure?"

"Your expectations for yourself are too high," he said. "People love your voice. They've come to see you. You don't have to be perfect."

He continued in this calming fashion until Miss White regained her confidence and her bitchiness. I didn't expect a thank you. She surprised me.

"Randall, why didn't you tell me your friend was so attractive?"

"Would you have believed me?"

"No." She beamed at Camden. "He's amazingly accurate, as well. Thank you for bringing him here."

"You're welcome."

"Even though I know you don't believe I need psychic assurance, I appreciate being taken seriously." She turned anxious eyes to Camden. "Can you stay?"

We'd left Elise safely at home with her mother. "I don't see why not," he said.

"And tomorrow? And for the rest of my concerts?"

"I'm pretty sure I can."

"If Diamond hasn't reconsidered by then, I'll bring him back," I said.

"At least an hour before each concert," Sherry said.

I found it odd that Camden hadn't picked up anything about the letters when he held her hand. "Who do you think is sending you threatening letters?" I asked Sherry.

She blinked as if she hadn't expected this question. "Some very disturbed person who hopes to ruin my career."

"Anyone in particular? What about Diamond? It seems suspicious she left all of a sudden."

"It couldn't possibly be Diamond. I gave her everything."

"Someone else who's left recently?"

"For the life of me, I can't keep decent backup singers, and the technicians are always giving me these lame excuses and quitting."

"Anyone you quarreled with?" I asked. "Anyone wanting more money?"

"I can't think of anyone. Why are you asking all these questions?"

"I'm a private investigator," I said. "Hire me and I can find out who's doing this."

She shook her head. "I've got too much on my mind right now. We'd have to discuss this later." She was much more interested in Camden. "Please stay with me until the concert starts. Once I'm on stage, I'm all right. It's the waiting beforehand that makes me crazy."

"I'll stay," he said, "but I promise, everything will go fine."

"Could I have your phone number? I'll give you mine. I want to be able to stay in touch."

"Yes, of course."

"Tickets," I said under my breath.

"Oh, yes, Miss White. Sherry. My wife and my friend Kary are huge fans. Would you happen to have any extra tickets for one of your concerts?"

"You can have whatever you like," she said. "I'll get you some for the Saturday concert."

Camden called Ellin to say he'd be staying for another hour. Sherry asked him to please sit with her in her dressing room and walk with her to the stage right before the show, which he did. Once she was on stage and into her first number, we were free to leave.

We were halfway down the hallway when Valerie Banner came running after us.

"Oh, my gosh, that was amazing!" she said. "It must be absolutely fascinating to have psychic abilities. I want to hear all about it."

"There's nothing to tell," Camden said.

"Oh, please! What does it feel like? Do you see things in color? How often do you have visions?"

"Camden, this is Valerie Banner, and she was obviously eavesdropping outside Sherry's door," I said. "She's way too persistent. You aren't going to get rid of her until you answer her questions."

"Occasionally, something pops into my mind," he said, "but usually, I have to touch an object, or shake someone's hand."

"Then what's it like?"

"I see whatever there is to see."

"Deaths? Murders? Accidents?"

"Sometimes."

"How does that feel?"

"Like death, murder, and accidents."

"What if you shake my hand?"

Camden held out his hand. "Okay."

Valerie hesitated and then took it. I guess she was expecting sparks and lightning, because she cringed. After a moment, she said, "Is it bad?"

"Nothing drastic," he said. "Your Uncle Jake's seen some strange things, though."

She gave a little squeal. "I was thinking of him! That's why I'm a journalist. His stories inspired me. What else did you see?"

"Your silver ring's behind the bureau."

"Wow! I've been looking for that. Did you see into my future?"

"Just the main things on your mind," he said. "That's it. That's the extent of my powers."

"Amazing" Valerie said. "But don't you feel you're wasted here in Parkland? You could be out doing something important, like being a spy for our country or something."

"That's not how I want to live."

From the few things he's said about his past, I figured Camden had been a really obnoxious teenager, a smartass know-it-all who actually did know it all. Not the best way to make or keep friends, and it had to be tough to look angelic and have raving devil visions inside that no one took seriously. People were gathering wood for a bonfire when he wised up, left his foster home, and took some years off wandering around, getting his act together.

"Would you come meet my Uncle Jake?" Valerie asked him. "He investigates stuff like this all the time. He's a reporter for the *Galaxy*."

"He's not friends with Tony Kenner, is he?" I asked.

She wrinkled her nose. "Gosh, no." To Camden she said, "This is so unbelievably cool. He's got to meet you, but I get the exclusive."

"There's no exclusive," Camden said. "There's no story."

Valerie looked at me. "But you're a real detective, right? You guys work together? I'll bet you've solved some really gruesome crimes, really strange stuff."

It would take years and possibly several books to explain the bizarre cases Camden and I had solved. "Nope," I said. "Plain ordinary crimes. Good night, Valerie."

"I still think there's a story here," she called after us.

When we got into the car, I said, "Did you pick up anything on the threatening letters?"

"No," Camden said. "Only a great deal of insecurity."

"Sherry doesn't seem as concerned as I thought she'd be," I

said. "She's a real drama queen, and threatening letters call for major drama."

"Maybe she isn't concerned. Maybe this kind of thing has happened before."

"I can believe that," I said.

*** 

Sometimes, for reasons I try to understand, Kary needed to sleep in her room. She liked her own space and liked being alone and independent.

Tonight wasn't one of those times.

The walls and curtains in my room are a nice shade of green, the furniture is old and dark brown, and the bed is large and very comfortable, especially when Kary decides to snuggle in next to me.

"I'm tired of thinking about school," she said. "Tell me about your new assignment. Is Sherry White as amazing as she sounds?"

I rearranged myself so she had more pillow. "The only thing amazing is how people put up with her tantrums."

"Oh, no, really? Is she a diva?"

"Diva's too tame. You'll have to invent a new word. Mega Diva. Divazilla." I explained how Sherry treated all the people who worked for her. "Apparently, somebody's had enough. She's getting threatening letters."

"Are you on the case?"

"I offered my services, but she said no. Fortunately, I had the perfect opportunity to put Camden on the inside track. Her personal psychic left, so he's filling in. He may be able to find out something."

"I've been worrying about having to move all day," Kary said. "I need a major distraction. Let me find out something about those letters."

"Of course. You know I'm always glad to have you help, and as for a major distraction—" I shifted to a more desirable position "—I know exactly what to do."

\*\*\*

I hadn't forgotten about Lindsey. Much later that night, I dreamed. I don't always dream about her, but she must have tuned into my concerns. Slowly the dream emerged. First, the faint happy cries of children in the playground, and then, out of the mist, Lindsey appeared. The breeze I could never feel lifted the hem of her white lace dress and played with the white ribbons in her hair.

"I don't want to move away," I said, "but it looks like that might happen."

*Don't worry, Daddy,* she said. *Wherever you are, I'm there, too.*

I felt an overwhelming sense of relief.

*And I have some good news,* she said. *Almost all the bad spirits are gone.*

"Almost all?"

*We think only five are left. You'll have to look out for them.*

"Any idea where they are and who they're in?" I asked. During my last encounter with one of these spirits, the evil creature had taken over a man whose dreams of being a magician had been turned into a fatal manipulation of everyone he met.

*No,* she said. *But there is something else you need to do. There is someone here who needs to cross over, and she can't leave until you help her.*

I'd done this kind of thing before. "Who is she? How can I

help? She's not being chased by one of those bad spirits, I hope."

*No, this is different,"* Lindsey said. *She died so long ago, but I can hear her music. It's your music, Daddy. Cam will find her, but you'll have to find the music.*

"My music? You mean ragtime? Traditional jazz?"

*You have to hurry. The place where she's dancing is going to be torn down. If you can't find the music before this happens, her spirit will never be with her family again.*

The dream began to fade. "Where is this place? Can you tell me anything else?"

Lindsey had vanished, but I heard her say one last thing.

*All she ever wanted to do was dance.*

# CHAPTER FOUR

*"Dancing on the Edge"*

T he mood Saturday morning was subdued. A light morning shower pattered at the window. Kary and I slept late and lingered for a long time before getting up. It was as if neither of us wanted to let go of each other or the calm shelter of the house.

Finally, Kary got up and shrugged into her white robe. While I took a shower, she made toast, the warm smell wafting up the stairs. I dressed in a tee shirt and jeans and stepped out onto the porch. Camden sat in the swing, his gaze miles past the roses growing over the porch railing, past the trees, their leaves glistening in the misty rain.

Elise, propped in his arm, snored tiny baby snores.

I sat down in a rocking chair. After a while, he rubbed his eyes and came back.

"Okay," I said. "I expect all my problems to be solved."

"Then you'll need to consult another psychic. The well is dry." He turned his gaze to me. "Lindsey can go with you."

As usual, he'd been aware of my dream. "Yes, that's a relief.

But she's given me another quest. There's another spirit who needs to move on, a spirit who'd better move on before wherever she's haunting is destroyed. Lindsey also said you could find her, but I'd have to find her music because it's my music."

"And that narrows it down to music written between 1889 and 1930," Camden said, "Which is quite a chunk of tunes."

"Yep. Any ideas?"

"No, the only thing I sensed was that Lindsey would always be with you." He smiled. "But you knew that."

"I did. It was nice to hear her say it, though. Did you hear the part about more evil spirits still running around? I'll bet one of them is the one you vanquished with your extra strength telekinesis. I award myself ten points for 'vanquished.'"

"'Vanquished' is worth only five points," he said, "and I hope that one is gone forever and not out for revenge."

Kary came out with a tray full of toast, butter, jam, two cups of coffee, and a plastic cup of cola for Camden. "Breakfast is served."

I hopped up to help her with the tray. I set it on the little wicker table between the rocking chairs and passed Camden his drink. "Toast for you?"

"I've already had breakfast, thanks."

Kary sat down in her rocker and picked up the butter knife. "Did I hear you mention spirits? Any more departed clients for the Randall Detective Agency?"

I reached for the toast. "Another ghost Lindsey wants me to help. Not much info on her yet, but we can't move out until I find her."

"That's as good an excuse as any."

"And the possibility of more evil spirits. Lindsey says there are five."

"Bring 'em on," she said.

Our conversation dwindled as we settled into our own thoughts. I listened to the hush of the rain on the leaves and the occasional swish of a car passing by. How many more times would we be able to enjoy breakfast on the porch, discussing cases and ghosts and whatever crazy thing happened, as it always did?

Things perked up when former tenant and Good Old Boy Rufus Jackson stopped by for a visit. He was happy to help himself to toast, and Kary brought an extra cup of coffee. He propped on the porch railing so he could face us and spit his ever-present tobacco juice over into the bushes. He'd heard about the possible move and had something to say about it, something characteristically Rufus.

"If I was you two, I'd turn it over and tickle it first."

I took a moment to figure this out. "Think about it, you mean? That's all we've been doing since the Mooresville job came up. If you can find Kary a teaching position in Parkland, then our problem is solved."

"Don't know nothin' about that," he said, "but Mooresville's a right long way from here. Can't say as I'd miss you, but not seeing Kary would put me in a sorry mood."

"We're all in a sorry mood," Kary said. "I'm going to have to say yes. It's too good a job to turn down."

"Then take it," Rufus said. "I got a truck. I'll help you move." He turned to Camden. "Reckon you'll be needin' more tenants, then."

"Don't move Kary and Randall out yet," he said. "There's still a chance."

"Wishful thinking, or you see something?"

"Everything's cloudy, as usual."

Kary leaned forward. "Cam, are you saying I shouldn't take the job?"

"Can you wait a little longer?"

"I told the Central Office in Mooresville I'd let them know Monday."

"If they could give you a little more time—" he paused. "I don't know. Things keep shifting."

Rufus chewed and spit. "Is it that telekinesis again? Hey, that'd be mighty handy for moving stuff. You could sail it into the truck. Look, Ma, no hands!"

To everyone's concern, that power's capacity for damage was growing. Camden gave him a look that suggested he'd like to sail Rufus somewhere. "No, it's not."

Kary's cell phone chimed and she answered it. She talked for a few minutes and then ended the call. "A friend of mine knows a realtor in Mooresville. I suppose it wouldn't hurt to have a look and see if there's anything reasonable available." She gathered the empty cups and put them on the tray. "I'm not going to sit around all day and worry. You let me know if Sherry White hires you, David."

"Sherry White?" Rufus said. "You workin' for her?"

"Not yet," I said. "Don't tell me you're a fan."

Rufus burst into a painfully nasal version of "Angel of Love" that woke the baby and made us laugh.

"Please stop," I said, as Elise yawned and stared at Rufus. "That's as bad as—as whatever Southern expression you want to use."

Kary had one. "You sing like a bellyached hog."

"Hawg," Rufus said. "If you're gonna say it, say it proper."

"Such a noise you can't hear your ears," Camden said.

Rufus gave a snort. "Y'all are always pickin' a crow."

"Enough," I said, still laughing. "Everybody stop."

"You started it," Rufus said. He held out his hand to Elise. She grasped one of his large fingers. "Sorry my purty lullaby woke you, tater tot." He wiggled his finger free and pulled himself up. "Let me know about the truck, Kary. Hope you won't need it."

\*\*\*

Kary went on to Mooresville with her friend. Toast and coffee wasn't quite enough breakfast for me, so I went in search of a snack and a change of pace. Camden and Elise were still swinging on the porch swing.

"You've got Sherry's number, right?" I asked Camden. "I want to call and see if she'll hire me."

"I'll text it to you."

I got a Coke and peanut butter crackers and sat down in one of the rocking chairs on the porch. Camden's text popped up and I called Sherry.

Her voice was just this side of desperate. "You're bringing Cam this afternoon, aren't you? He needs to be here by one."

"I'll get him there," I said. "Have you received any more letters?"

"No, thank God."

"I'd like to find out who's behind this," I said. "When could we meet and discuss your case?"

She hesitated. "I'm resting and meditating today, Mr. Randall. Why don't we meet when you and Cam come to the auditorium?"

"That's fine, thanks. We'll see you an hour before the performance." I ended the call.

"So you're in?" Camden asked.

"Almost. I figure if I'm hauling you over there every day, I might as well get in some detecting along with my security gig, and with Tony Kenner in the picture, I know something shady's going on. I wouldn't put it past him to blackmail Sherry."

Just then, a cheery little voice said, "Hello, Cam. Hello, David."

The voice came from the hedge that separated Camden's house from his neighbor's. Lily Wilkes popped out, beaming, as usual. Lily appeared to be in her thirties and had an odd fascination with UFOs. She claimed to have been abducted several times. The aliens kept bringing her back, so that told me something right there. She was cute and petite, with puffy white hair, sort of like the Elf Queen of Cotton. She was always pleasant. But spacey—! You could put an entire galaxy in her head with room left over for a spare nebula or two. As leader of a band of space cadets, the ASG, Abductees Support Group, she always asked Camden to come to the meetings, and he always did. None of the members lived in the real world, but he never tried to convince them otherwise. He listened to their stories, which is all they really wanted.

Lily hopped through the hedge and up onto the porch dressed in her usual fashion, which was Grab Bag Deluxe. She wore a lacy apron with a pattern of dancing birds over something I'll call a jumper for lack of a better description. She also had on one of her hats. This one looked as if it had been a sailor hat in a past life. Lily had decorated the hat with a wad of Christmas tinsel and some faded artificial daisies. She carried a wooden box, which she held out to Camden.

"Cam, could you feel these, please, and tell me what you think?"

"Would you like to hold Elise while I do that?"

"I'd love to."

Lily sat down in a rocking chair and carefully took Elise. Camden opened the box. Light caught on the spires of a dozen glittery glass objects. "Where did you get these?"

"The Dimity House," she said. "The new owner gave us permission to take whatever we wanted."

Dimwitty House was more like it. The former owner, Elias Burke, had been a real crackpot, the kind of man who hoards aluminum foil and string. "Who's the new owner?" I asked.

"A Mr. Jason Frost. He's going to remodel the whole house. At least he's not tearing it down."

"He let you salvage stuff?"

"Mr. Burke was a member of our group. It's in his will that the ASG have first pick of his belongings. There wasn't a lot the cats hadn't ruined, though."

"Cats?"

"Mr. Burke had about fifty cats."

Camden took out one of the crystals. "These are from an old chandelier."

"That's right," Lily said. "Unfortunately, most of them are broken. The chandelier fell years ago, and Mr. Burke never put it back up."

I was still shuddering at the thought of fifty cats. "Too busy working the can opener."

Lily watched Camden, her expression hopeful. "So what do you think? Do any of them have any beneficial powers? Gosh, be careful, though. Some of the broken ones are pretty sharp."

Camden avoided the broken pieces, his attention drawn to one of the larger whole crystals. His expression was thoughtful as his fingers smoothed the bright surface. He was miles away. "The house was so beautiful. So many parties. So many dances. Something not quite right."

Attracted by the shiny objects, Elise reached over and touched a crystal. She drew her little hand back.

*Not good,* came her voice. *Not good, Daddy.*

Camden looked at his daughter in amazement. "You see it, too?" She gazed at him solemnly.

"What?" Lily said. "Oh, my gosh, is Elise already psychic?"

"You now get two for the price of one," I said.

"Wow! What did she see?"

Camden continued to smooth the crystal. "I'm not sure." Elise reached for it again, but he handed the crystal to Lily. "You might want to put this one away."

Lily's eyes stayed wide. She took the crystal as if it might explode. "Thanks."

"I don't think it's dangerous. It just doesn't feel right. The others are okay, though. No vibes."

She nodded and put the crystal back in the box. "Thanks. Well, I'd better go. See you later."

"Good job, Elise," I said, but she'd gone back into regular Baby Mode, waving her little arms and cooing.

Camden gave her a hug and kissed the top of her silky blond head. "When her little sister and brother arrive, then you'll see some fireworks."

"Do we get a few years in between when nothing peculiar happens?"

"Dream on," he said.

\*\*\*

The special concert for the Wishing Star Foundation was at one o'clock that afternoon, and I'd promised Sherry to bring Camden an hour before. He buckled Elise in her car seat in the Fury's back seat, and I drove to the auditorium parking lot, where Sherry had reserved a space for us. Camden arranged the baby in her carry pouch that I called a front pack. I showed the policeman on guard my pass, and we found our way to Sherry's dressing room.

The minute she saw him, Sherry ran and grasped Camden's hands. "There are so many sick children coming today. I have to do my very best for them. Please tell me everything will be all right. This may be the last concert some of them ever get to hear. It has to be perfect."

"It's all right, Sherry," he said. "No matter what you do, they'll love it."

"But my manager said some might even be in hospital beds. It's too much."

"You can do it."

This wasn't the time to discuss the Phantom Letter Writer, so I took a stroll around the stage area. The band instruments were in place and one of the technicians was doing a last minute test of the microphones for the backup singers. The lower level of the auditorium slowly filled with children in wheelchairs and beds, their caregivers by their sides. The Wishing Star Foundation funded events for terminally ill children, and apparently, all of these kids wanted to hear Sherry White. I had to admit that performing for this kind of audience would add a certain amount of pressure, but surely Sherry White had done this dozens of times during her career. At any rate, Camden would calm her down.

Sure enough, when I came back to the dressing room, Sherry

had Elise on her lap, holding her close and smiling.

"Elise is such a doll," she said. "I feel so calm holding her."

"We dust her with sleeping powder," I said. No need to mention to Sherry that Elise was probably sending out soothing rays in her own little psychic way.

Camden offered her the carry pouch. "Do you want to wear her during the concert?"

She laughed again. "Now wouldn't that create a stir? No, thank you. I'm fine now, really."

"About those letters," I said.

She gave me a glare. "I'm in a good place right now, Randall. I don't want to talk about that."

"Fine. Just say the word. I'll handle it."

"I don't really think that's necessary."

"You want them stopped, don't you?"

"Of course."

"Randall's an excellent detective, Sherry," Camden said. "If you're worried about harmful publicity, he'll keep everything very discreet."

"I'm sure you're right," she said. "Maybe we can discuss this after the concert. Cam, I want you out front with me. All these children—I need to be strong."

During the hour-long concert, I kept backstage, but nothing suspicious happened. From the sound of the cheers and applause, Sherry hadn't disappointed her young fans. If she needed Camden's presence to feel confident, I understood that. What I didn't understand was her reluctance to hire me, or anyone, for that matter, who could take care of the letter problem.

I took another stroll around and into Sherry's dressing room. I surprised Valerie Banner, who was rooting in the drawers of the dressing table. She straightened as if I'd poked her with something sharp.

"Oh! Gosh! I guess this looks bad, doesn't it? I wasn't doing anything, really."

"Aren't you supposed to be out front interviewing kids for your magazine?" I asked.

Her eyes darted around the room as if she was looking for an escape route. "Uh, yeah, I'm getting to that, but I thought I saw someone sneaking around back here."

"You're the only one sneaking around back here."

Behind her back, something crackled in her hand. She tried to keep bluffing, but her blush gave her away. "Okay, I found something, but it's mine, an exclusive, got that?"

"Hand it over."

"I'll show it to you."

She held the paper so I could read it. It was a yellow piece of paper with "Die" written in thick black ink.

"Where did you find this?" I asked.

"Stuck in her mirror."

"It's evidence. It needs to go to the police, or better yet, let Camden hold it."

She shook her head and stuffed the paper in her shoulder bag. "I found it. It's for my story."

"Damn it, Valerie, it could tell us who's doing this," I said. "You'll get the credit, if that's what you want."

"I don't trust you."

"How do I know you didn't put it there yourself?"

She looked properly horrified. "Me?"

"That's what I'm going to tell the police. In fact, I'm going to tell them right now."

I started out and she grabbed my arm. "Wait! All right, I'll hand it over, but you promise me I'll get the story on this."

"You'll get your story if it's so important."

She pulled the crumpled paper from her bag. "You think we should show it to Miss White?"

"Yes, and the police will need it."

Valerie reluctantly handed it over.

After the concert, Sherry actually took time to speak to some of the children. I could tell this meant a lot to them, and she looked almost attractive as she smiled and signed autographs. I gave the paper to Camden, who frowned and said, "What was Valerie doing with this?"

"You get anything?"

"Just Valerie, wildly excited about a story."

"Damn. I thought maybe she planted it in the dressing room, hoping Sherry would find it."

"She didn't plant it." He smoothed the paper. "Was it in Sherry's mirror?"

"Yep."

"That's all I'm getting, sorry."

We waited in Sherry's dressing room until she had greeted all her young fans. She came in looking tired but happy. I really hated to spoil her day.

"Sherry, Valerie found this stuck in your mirror."

Her hand shook as she took the paper. "Not another one!"

"Do you recognize the handwriting? The paper? Anything?"

"No. Who could be doing this?"

"That's what I want to find out."

Finally my message got through. She gave me a long measuring look and then said, "All right. You're hired. Find out who's doing this and make them stop."

\*\*\*

At the police station I explained to Jordan why the letter had Camden's fingerprints on it as well as mine and Valerie Banner's.

"Miss White has hired me to find out who's doing this," I said.

Usually Jordan objects to having me in the way, but in this instance, he was glad someone else was running interference. "My first guess would be Valerie Banner," he said. "She looks innocent, but I know her Uncle Jake. He'd do anything for a story."

"Even write threatening notes for his niece to find accidentally on purpose?"

"He's quite a character, but this doesn't seem to be his style."

When Camden held Valerie's hand, he said this Uncle Jake had seen some strange things. "Is he a legitimate reporter?"

"If you call the *Galaxy News Weekly* a legitimate newspaper."

Well, this was an interesting coincidence and one I would explore.

# CHAPTER FIVE

*"Dancing on My Own"*

I stopped by the stage to interview the crew, the technicians, the band, and the roadies.

One crew member rolled up a long extension cord. "Miss White can be difficult, but I've worked with worse. Most of us don't know what goes on backstage. We've got too much work to do out here."

"But all of you have heard about the letters?" I asked.

"Yeah, it's too bad, but she's made a lot of people mad over the years. I think somebody's just trying to scare her."

"Any idea who might be playing such a mean joke?"

"Not me, man. I gotta keep this job."

The members of the band had similar opinions. I found them in their dressing room, getting ready to go out. "We aren't allowed in her dressing room," the drummer said with a wry grin. "We do our job, and then we find a nice restaurant, maybe sit in with a local group. It's not a bad gig. We've been with her for a while. We know how she is."

"I understand her latest album didn't do as well as expected,"

I said.

"You never know. When that new teen sensation came on the scene, it blew everybody off the charts. The competition's stiff these days."

"Would you say her career's in danger?"

He shrugged. "It's possible. She doesn't pack 'em in like she used to. I wouldn't say her career's over, but it definitely isn't the same."

In the next dressing room, I was invited in by the backup singers, three attractive women who were also planning their evening activities. Sherry was an equal opportunity employer, for one woman was short, white, and plump, one was an Asian woman, thin and willowy, and the other was a tall black woman with rows of beads in her braided hair, who introduced herself as Clarissa. The women had changed from their sparkly show outfits to casual shirts and jeans. I apologized for interrupting them, introduced myself, and asked them how the tour was going.

Clarissa sighed. "Honey, we'd all like Miss White to get all the love and attention she needs. As long as she's happy, we're happy."

"Is she ever happy?" I asked.

"Oh, yes. You wait till she's out there in front of an audience. She loves it, and the people, they love her back. I think the experience is so wonderful she can't live in the real world. She's got to have that applause, that adoration. Now, I love performing, but I can do without it. Going to, at the end of this tour. I've had it."

"So have we," the short woman said.

"You three are going to quit?"

"Got me another offer, and I'm taking it."

"Does Sherry know this?"

"No," the Asian woman said, "and you'd better not tell her.

Besides, even with her reputation, there's singers lined up to work with her. Now that she's stopped blacklisting people, she won't have trouble getting some more. I think we're the fifth or sixth set she's gone through in the past year. We belong to a select club, the Sherry White Survivors. There's tons of us."

"So what you're saying is she has tons of enemies," I said.

She laughed. "There's a million people who could've sent those letters. You got your work cut out for you."

"What did you mean by blacklisting people?" I asked. "Can she do that?"

"She used to have a lot more clout than she does now," Clarissa explained. "There for a while, she did keep people from working. She'd just give a director a call and say, if you hire so and so, I'm not singing at your gala, I'm not recording your song, or whatever. She had a lot of power. Then all those producers and directors wised up. Now everyone knows about her temper."

This opened up a world of suspects. "Anyone whose career was completely ruined?"

"I'm sure a lot of people never worked again."

"But you're not afraid she might do this to you?"

The three of them exchanged little smirks. "Like I said, she *had* a lot of power," Clarissa said. "Not anymore."

\*\*\*

I went back to Sherry's dressing room. She had Elise on her lap and looked a lot calmer.

I got right to the point. "Sherry, is there anyone you've black-listed lately?"

The calm look disappeared. "Who told you that? I never black-listed anyone!"

"Okay, is there anyone you've kept from working? Maybe made a phone call to a certain director or producer?"

"Based on their performance, there have been people I could not recommend, if that's what you mean."

"I'd like their names."

She gave me another long considering gaze. "I'll see what I can do." She hugged Elise once more and handed her to Camden. "I want to hold her all day, but I need to rest. Thank you so much." She picked up an envelope from her dressing table. "Oh, and here are your tickets for next Saturday's concert, Randall."

I put the envelope in my pocket. "Thanks. We'll see you later."

When Camden, Elise, and I got out to the parking lot, Valerie was waiting by my car.

"Am I in the clear?" she asked. "Can I go ahead with the story?"

"Sure," I said. Let her think she's off the hook. "Did Jordan talk to you?"

"That giant policeman? Yes, I told him everything. He doesn't think I did it." She didn't add, "So there!" but I could tell she wanted to.

"Okay, I believe you," I said.

"Great! What about the letter? Do you have it?"

"The police want to keep it."

"Shoot! I was going to print that, too, but you startled me before I could take a picture of it."

"Kind of hard to forget one word."

Ellin could take my head off with a glare. Valerie gave it her best shot, but she had a long way to go to be in Ellin's class. "Very funny."

"Good-by, Valerie."

She wasn't about to give up. "Cam, did you get anything from the letter? Any psychic messages?"

"Nothing helpful," he said.

She bounced on her toes. "So, are you two on the case?"

"Randall's on the case. I'm just playing security blanket for Sherry."

I got into the car. "Stop talking to her and maybe she'll go away."

Valerie set her mouth in a firm line. "Not me. I'm never going away."

"Well, we are. Come on, Camden."

He buckled Elise in her car seat and got in. As we drove away, we could see Valerie Banner, arms folded, glaring after the car.

"What do you think?" I asked. "Is she going to cause trouble?"

"She's got a crush on you," Camden said.

"Hell, who doesn't?"

Elise made her chuckling noise. I looked back at her, and she gave me an innocent wide-eyed gaze. "Just what I need, a couple of psychic comedians. Tell me how you arrived at that conclusion."

"Let's just say the Big Story is not the only thing she's hoping to score."

"Oh, I plan to get close, but not in the way she's hoping," I said. "I have a pretty good idea she's writing these letters, and all this gee-whiz girl reporter routine is just a cover."

Camden grinned and so did Elise.

I tried to glare and ended up grinning, too. "Next time, I'm leaving both of you home."

***

I took Camden and Elise back to 302 Grace and called the office of the *Galaxy News Weekly*. Now that I was officially on the case, Valerie Banner was Suspect Number One. The fact that her Uncle Jake and Tony Kenner both worked for the tabloid was an interesting connection. And Valerie and Kenner had been at the auditorium at the same time. Was she supposed to let him in, and I happened to foil their plan?

I didn't think the *Galaxy* was classy enough to have a receptionist, but it did. She was willing to give me Kenner's cell phone number, but explained he probably wouldn't be available to take any calls.

"Is Kenner doing a story on Sherry White?" I asked.

"I don't know, sir. I do know he has a big interview coming up with one of the hottest new bands in the area." She lowered her voice. "We suspect one of the band members is an alien."

"How about Jake Banner? Do you have a contact number for him? I think I saw Bigfoot in the woods behind my house."

She was happy to give me his number. "We can always use a good Bigfoot story."

"Great," I said. "Thank you."

***

Neither Kenner nor Uncle Jake answered the phone, but Jake's had a cheery voice message that said, "Yo! Cruising around Stonehenge in my UFO. Leave a message."

"Got a hot tip on Bigfoot," I said and left my name and number.

On to my next suspect, Sherry's former psychic. The Psychic Service had a psychic named Sapphire. Maybe they had a Diamond, too.

I gave the Psychic Service main office a call, and sure enough, they had a Sapphire, an Emerald, and a Topaz, but no Diamond. Then I decided to call the Psychic Service Network studio. Maybe Ellin would know.

"Odd you should mention that," Ellin said when I asked about Diamond. "We had a call from a woman named Diamond today, looking for a job. She's supposed to come in for an interview."

"Did she leave an address or phone number?"

"Wait a minute." I heard paper rustle, and then Ellin spoke to one of the hosts. "Reg, what's this note here about a telethon?"

Reg Haverson, her warmup man and occasional host for the PSN shows, was always scheming for more air time and had many useless ideas. I heard his voice. "It works for PBS."

"Yes, and it drives everyone crazy. We are not going to have a telethon."

A psychic telethon. All you have to do is imagine the amount of money you'd send.

Ellin came back to me. "She's staying at the Mid-Town Hotel, Randall."

"Thanks," I said, and just to annoy her, added, "Tell Reg to keep up the good work."

\*\*\*

The Parkland Mid-Town Hotel was an older hotel, but very classy, with potted palm trees in the foyer, a grand sweep of staircase, and an elegant little coffee shop overlooking Windom Park.

Diamond agreed to meet me in the lobby and accepted an offer of coffee. She was a small woman with close-cut black hair in jagged bangs and a tattoo of roses and vines twisting down one arm. With her large eyes, small nose, and rounded chin, she reminded me of a Japanese anime heroine. She was just as feisty and vengeful as one, too.

After the waitress brought our coffee, Diamond leaned forward and spoke with barely contained anger. "Sherry White is a horrible woman. I'm surprised I have any powers left after dealing with her for so long. I'm surprised she didn't drain me completely. I hear she already has another psychic. He'd better get out while he can."

"Are you aware of the threats Sherry White has received?" I asked.

"Oh, yes. She blames me for not foreseeing such things. She said I should have known and prevented them, I should have warned her." She sat back as if amazed by such treachery. "She has no idea how the psychic mind operates. I don't see everything. How could I possibly know about those letters when she kept me in such a state?"

"Did you receive any impressions from the letters?"

"I would have been happy to, but she burned them before I had a chance. She has a horrible temper. There's no dealing with her." She took a sip of coffee. "She came from a very poor background, you know, and it's simply a case of too much too soon. She's been given everything and told she's a goddess, and now everyone caters to her whims."

"But she can't function without a psychic."

"Low self-esteem, that's all there is to it."

Diamond should have been a psychiatrist instead of a psychic

"Do you have any idea who might be sending her these letters?"

"Probably some lunatic fan trying to get her attention," she said.

"So you don't think she's in any real physical danger?"

"Why bother with that when you can psyche her out? It doesn't take much to set her off. That's why her ex left her. Someone's just trying to rattle her."

She took another sip and looked down into her cup. I wondered if she was attempting to read coffee grounds instead of tea leaves. Apparently, the coffee had nothing to reveal because she returned her gaze to me.

"I can't say I'm sorry. Now that I'm away from her, I feel much better, but it's impossible for me to work up any sympathy for her. You've seen her in action, haven't you?"

"Lots of entertainers are high-strung," I said. "She seems genuinely frightened by the letters."

Diamond stirred her coffee and made a humpf noise to express her lack of concern.

"Tell me about her ex-husband," I said.

"Mitch Stratton. Last I heard he was shooting a documentary in China. He always loved photography and loved to travel, so he enjoyed the concert tours, for a while, anyway, until he found out what a monster she was. Do you know she had the gall to criticize his acting? Have you ever seen *her* act? And he had a company for a while called Crystal Films that went nowhere fast. Guess why? I'm glad he escaped her clutches."

"You're saying Sherry sabotaged his acting career? So he might be sending these letters."

"Oh, he has his own film company now, and he's doing what he loves to do. He's a nice guy who didn't deserve to be treated the way Sherry treated him. He'd had enough of Sherry, so he got out. I wouldn't think he'd want anything to do with her. Ever."

"How about someone Sherry fired?"

Diamond laughed. "Oh, my God, it would take forever to list the names! She fires people every day, every hour. The weird thing is there are always hundreds lined up to take their places. She goes through backup singers like potato chips."

"How about her agent, her production company?"

"Same thing."

"So there's not one constant in her whole life?"

Diamond gave me an arch look. "Just that she's a bitch and doesn't care."

The waitress stopped by to see if we'd like a refill and perhaps some pie. Diamond said she'd like a piece of apple pie and more coffee. I took another cup. Talking with Diamond was like getting a free case of heartburn. I'll admit Sherry was difficult, but this world-wide loathing seemed out of proportion.

"Is there anyone who likes her?" I asked. "Her fans are crazy about her."

Diamond gave me a look that said, you don't get it, do you? "Her fans adore her because they've never actually met her and they're not likely to. You see how she keeps herself aloof. She'll wave and blow kisses and let a few take pictures, but she really doesn't like them. She's told me how they keep her from having a normal life, how she can't go to the movies or to the grocery store, how she feels like a prisoner in this society and how the news magazines are always telling lies. The fans truly made her what she is, but she honestly despises them."

"Why doesn't she quit, then? She's certainly rich enough. Stop giving concerts for a while. Buy a nice little Caribbean island and relax."

"She's addicted to applause, to the cheers and the adulation. I don't think she could live without it."

This was the same thing Clarissa had told me.

The waitress returned with Diamond's apple pie and an offer of more coffee. We both said no, thanks. After she left, I picked up the thread. "So Sherry's not thinking of retiring any time soon?"

"She hit a slump last year when record sales weren't as high as she'd like, but with this latest record, I don't see any signs of her slowing down. Of course, I predicted all this, but she barely listened to me, she was in such a fever over declining sales."

"Why do you think sales were down?"

Diamond smiled a thin humorless smile. "I don't think. I know. A glut of divas." She laughed a short laugh. "That's good, isn't it? A flock of geese, a glut of divas? Way too many female superstars crowding each other out of the charts. I told Sherry to wait before issuing 'My Heart's Full For You,' but she didn't listen, and the record didn't do as well against her rivals'."

"'Angel of Love' is doing well."

Diamond was determined to take all credit for Sherry's success "That's because I told her to bring it out right before Christmas. Christmas, angel, it makes sense, doesn't it? Now the record's a monster hit and all she can do is yell at me." She hacked at her piece of pie as if it were responsible for Sherry's unfaithfulness. "I can tell when I'm not wanted or appreciated. I don't have to be psychic for that."

I'd had my quota of bitterness for the day. I checked my watch. "I have another appointment. Thanks for your time."

"No problem," she said. "I'll be in town for a while if you have any more questions. I'm hoping to get a job with the Psychic Service Network. You know anything about it?"

"A little."

"A pretty good size operation, from the look of things. I hear the producer's tough, but she can't be any harder to work for than Sherry White."

I thought it best not to comment on this.

"Tell the new psychic to watch his back," Diamond said. "Is he good-looking?"

What was she on about now? "Most women think so."

Diamond gave a sniff to show how little she cared. "Then tell him to watch his front, too. Miss White thinks she's a real sex-pot."

No real good answer to that, either. I decided on, "Thanks for your help."

"My pleasure. Thanks for the pie and coffee. She gave me a measuring stare. "I might have some more information for you later. My room number's four thirty-eight."

"I'll keep that in mind."

"If you do, I'll know it."

These psychics.

I started back out through the foyer and saw a familiar figure lurking behind one of the palm trees.

"Come on out, Valerie."

She casually circled the tree as if to say, "I meant to be here."

"You found Diamond," she said.

"It wasn't difficult."

"What did she say?"

"You can ask her yourself."

"She's the letter-writer, isn't she? She hates Sherry, and this is a way she can get back at her."

"Yep, you've solved the case. We can all go home now."

Valerie's eyes surprised me by narrowing. I wasn't sure they could. "You think you're so smart. I'm going to find out who's behind these letters, with or without your help."

"Without, please."

She immediately changed tactics. "David, we should work together. We'd make a great team."

"I already have a partner, remember?"

She swung her shoulder bag around so fast, I thought she was going to smack me with it, but she was angling for her phone. "Well, I'm going up to talk to her."

"Good luck."

# CHAPTER SIX

### *"Dancin' Away With My Heart"*

I didn't have another suspect, but I did have an overwhelming urge to see Kary and get her caught up on the case. I sent her a text to find out where she was, and she replied she was home from Mooresville.

It was past six o'clock and I was hungry. Kary was seated in a porch rocking chair halfway through a plate of lasagna.

"I waited on you," she said, which was a running joke. No one waited on anyone when Camden made lasagna for supper.

I took out the envelope and handed it to her. "I come bearing good news. Thanks to Camden agreeing to be Sherry's new psychic, you and Ellin have tickets for Sherry White in Concert next Saturday night."

"I'm not sure I've earned a ticket," she said. "I haven't had a chance to investigate those threatening letters yet. Anything new on the case?"

I told her about Sherry's legion of haters, including her ex-husband and her ex-psychic. "This plot also has ties to the *Galaxy News Weekly* and the *Herald's* 'New Faces' junior reporter, Valerie

Banner. Plus a lot of folks have decided to desert the *S.S. Sherry White.*"

I went to the kitchen and opened the stove to scoop up a manly portion of the lasagna. I brought my plate and a Coke out to the porch and sat down in another rocking chair.

We ate in silence for a few minutes. Kary took a sip of her cola. "I looked at several houses in Mooresville that might suit us."

"Okay."

A few more minutes of silence, and Kary changed the subject. "Ellin must be thrilled that Cam's the new psychic. Is he going on tour with Sherry?"

"Ellin will be sitting next to you at the Saturday concert. You can get all the details."

"You've had a busy afternoon," she said. "Is there anything I could do to help?"

"Become a full-fledged member of the Randall Detective Agency. The pay's not great, but the benefits are astounding."

She feigned being offended. "I am a full-fledged member."

"All this time wasted at school. Forget this altruistic notion you have of molding young minds."

"'Altruistic.' My heavens. Isn't that worth twenty points?"

"It's far nobler to solve dastardly crimes and get murderers off the streets. Plus teacher pay isn't that great, either, is it? Think it over—no, turn it over and tickle it."

She took another drink of cola and set the can by her chair. "Thank you, but I have to say no for two reasons. One, I am, as you know, amazingly independent."

"Yes, I know this."

"And two, much as I hate to say this, the Randall Detective Agency isn't always lucky enough to have Sherry White cases."

"Ouch."

"Admit it," she said in a teasing tone. "Sometimes even Cam makes more money than you."

"It is sadly true that my fortunes go up and down," I said. "But I could get a second job. I know how to tend bar."

"You've told me you hate it."

"Rufus could get me on with his construction crew." When she laughed, I said, "Now what's so funny about that? I could learn to drive a bulldozer."

She leaned over and gave me a kiss on the cheek. "Of course you could."

I thought of something else. "How would you feel about seeking life advice from Diamond? You may be able to find out something useful about her relationship with Sherry."

"You think she's the letter writer?"

"She's certainly angry enough. Since she's just been fired, she'd probably welcome a customer."

From the way Kary's eyes sparkled she was planning a disguise. "I'll do it."

A neighbor waved from her convertible as she drove down Grace Street, radio cranked up full blast.

"Oh, listen," Kary said. "'Angel of Love.'"

"Sherry White's latest ode to the elevators of America."

"Which I'm going to hear her sing in person. That's something to look forward to. Thanks so much, David."

The screen door squeaked and Camden came out, Elise asleep on his shoulder. He sat down on the porch swing. "Sherry has called ten times."

"Did she give you a list of people she's destroyed?" I asked.

"No." He pushed his hair out of his eyes and carefully shifted

Elise to his other shoulder.

"Have you talked with any of the potential new PSN sponsors?" I asked.

"Not yet. Do you think that would help?"

"Ellin said she needed more, and it's always useful to have extra favors on hand."

"That's true." Elise gave a little hiccup and settled back to sleep. "I know you're working on Sherry's case. Would you have time to take me around to the sponsors?"

"Sure," I said. "We'll find the time. Besides, how long will it take for you to charm them? Ten minutes? Fifteen? Just tell the women they'll meet tall dark handsome strangers, and tell the men they're going to be rich. Easy."

He turned his attention to Kary. "How was your trip to Mooresville? Are you all right?"

"As all right as I can be at the moment," she said.

"Can't you see anything that would get her a job here?" I asked Camden. "Why don't you fire up your telekinesis and go over to the Central Office and make them give her a position?"

"It's way too destructive to be let loose," he said. "You know that."

"You don't think flinging chairs around and making daggers out of pencils would be convincing?"

"I think it would get me put away, and then Kary would definitely not get a job."

"We should pool our vast resources and build another school in Parkland," I said. "No, here's a better idea. Maybe when I catch the letter writer, Sherry will build another school for me. That's it. Problem solved."

"I don't think she's that wealthy," Camden said.

"Really?"

"When she was holding Elise, she told me about her child-hood. She and I have something in common. Like me, Sherry doesn't know who her father was, and her mother couldn't provide for a baby. Unlike me, though, she was adopted by a family who loved her and encouraged her talent. They weren't very well off. Practically every penny Sherry makes she sends back to the town where she grew up, trying to make a difference for the children there. She said she didn't want any other kids to have to grow up wanting things their parents couldn't afford."

"Diamond mentioned that Sherry grew up poor," I said. "If it's so important that her concerts and recordings make money, you'd think she'd be nice and polite to the people who are trying to help her."

"I don't think she's aware of that. She's frantic. She feels her career is slipping away, and she doesn't know what to do about it."

Elise whimpered a little. Camden rocked her and patted her back. "It's okay, baby. It's just a dream."

"She's dreaming already?"

"Sometimes she dreams and sometimes she sees things," he said. "It'll be a while before she understands what all the pictures mean."

"Any signs of baby telekinesis?"

"Not yet."

\*\*\*

After supper, Kary called Diamond and set up an appointment for a psychic reading. I'd hoped Sherry would call with that list of names she'd promised, but I didn't hear from her. After a while,

Kary went upstairs, no doubt to plan her disguise, and Camden and I diverted ourselves by watching a truly bad science fiction movie, *First Spaceship to Venus*.

When Denny came in from the Pyramid, he was all decked out in a black wig that flipped up, a white ruffled blouse, and black Capri pants. He looked like an industrial strength Mary Tyler Moore. He watched a little of the movie with us before heading upstairs to get his beauty sleep. Camden was in the kitchen fixing a bottle for Elise when Ellin came home. I asked if she'd interviewed Diamond.

She put her briefcase on the bench of the hall tree. "She's coming in Monday."

"It would be very helpful if you hired her."

"Helpful in what way?"

I rarely asked Ellin for a favor, but this coincidence was too good to pass up. "I'm sure she told you she's Sherry White's ex-psychic advisor. Sherry hired me to find out who's been sending threatening letters. Diamond's a likely suspect."

"You think she might let something slip?"

"And you'd be there to catch it."

Ellin gave me an unreadable stare. "All right," she said. "We need another psychic for our help line. I'll give her a try."

"Thanks," I said.

Camden came around the corner from the kitchen. Elise, on his shoulder, gave a resounding burp. "Atta girl," he told her. "Have you had supper?" he asked Ellin. "There's some leftover lasagna."

She gave them both a kiss. "Right now, I want to hop in the shower."

"Would you like some company? Randall can hold Elise."

Elise was already leaning towards me. "Be glad to," I said.

Camden went back up the stairs with Ellin. I took Elise into the island and we sat down in the faded blue armchair. The baby snuggled back against me, content.

"How about if you and I just stay here?" I asked her. "Everybody else can move on out." I wasn't surprised to hear her little voice in my mind.

*Okay, Dave.*

# CHAPTER SEVEN

### *"Just One Dance"*

Sunday morning, Kary and Camden went to church, Ellin took Elise to see her grandmother, and I started my search for Mitch Stratton. A Google search located a web address at www.images.com. The website showed pictures of a tall, pleasant-looking dark-haired man with a video camera on his shoulder. The brief bio read, "Mitch Stratton is a world traveler and photographer dedicated to documenting people and cultures that might otherwise go unnoticed." Here was Mitch talking with Bedouin tribesmen in the Sahara. Here was Mitch on a boat in the Amazon, aiming his lens at a group of fishermen. According to the website, he was currently in Beijing with his company, shooting a documentary on rice farmers. There was no mention of Sherry White. However, at the bottom of the page was a message to donors and subscribers. "Due to unforeseen circumstances, 'Rice Farmers in Crisis' will be my last film. As of next month, Images will no longer be in business and the website will shut down. I wish to thank everyone who has supported me on this incredible journey."

Images welcomed comments, so I sent an email including my

phone number expressing sympathy and offering to donate to any unpaid expenses for "Rice Farmers in Crisis." That should get a reply.

I had the Sunday edition of the *Parkland Herald* on my desk. On page three under "New Faces" was Valerie's story about Sherry White's latest difficulties, stating that the popular singer was being plagued by mysterious threatening letters. Since the folks at the *Herald* and I had worked together on several cases, I was on good terms with Bill Rutherford, Valerie's boss, and had his home number.

"I have a couple of questions regarding Valerie Banner," I said.

"Oh, yes, Valerie," Bill said. "A very eager young woman, very conscientious. "

"Someone who'd do anything for a story?"

"You're thinking of her uncle, Jake Banner. Valerie's trying to avoid that kind of investigative reporting."

From what I'd seen, Valerie thought otherwise. "I thought 'New Faces' was on the softer side of the news."

"It's true we do a lot of features about celebrities, but we also like to write about hometown heroes, and we like to uncover shady happenings, scams, things people should be warned about. Restaurants that don't make the grade, for instance. Our readers are very concerned about that."

"Did you assign Valerie the Sherry White story?" I asked.

"Yes. When I learned that Sherry was going to be staying in Parkland for a week, I knew this was an excellent opportunity to get an in-depth story. I had no idea Valerie would stumble upon this mysterious letter writer. Now that's been a real attention-grabber."

"Something Valerie might make up to get headlines?"

"I don't believe she's capable of that."

"You said she was eager and conscientious."

Bill chuckled. "That's not what I meant by capable. As a writer, she has limitations. But I like her enthusiasm."

It was true that Valerie's article was very dry. "So what about the Sherry White story? Is she still assigned to it?"

"I've asked Valerie to continue to follow the story," he said. "We'll keep our readers aware of what's going on, we just won't be as lurid as the *Galaxy*."

Nothing could be as lurid as the *Galaxy*. "Do you know why Sherry's staying in Parkland for a week?" I asked. "We're a big city, but we're not New York or L.A."

"It's my understanding that she's here to take some time off for meditation."

Sherry herself had mentioned meditation. She did not strike me as a woman who could sit in a calm state, humming softly. I thanked Bill and went online. There were several spas in Parkland that offered group meditation. I called each one, inquiring about Sherry White. I figured the spa she chose would be pleased to have such an important guest. Luckily, I was right on my third phone call.

"Yes, we're honored to have Miss White join us for the Soothing Waters Seminar here at the Healing Day Spa," an equally soothing woman's voice informed me. "However, in respect for her need for privacy, we cannot discuss details."

"I understand," I said. "Could you tell me more about the seminar?"

"All the information is on our website, sir, Healing Day Spa dot com, but I'm afraid we are full at the moment."

"That's okay," I said. "I'll catch the next one."

I read all about the seminar on the web page. It sounded way too calm for me, but if Sherry needed something like that to keep her from exploding, then I was glad she was participating. As I scrolled down the page, I thought this was exactly the kind of thing Kary would be thrilled to do, infiltrate the spa and chat with all the people, finding out little things that sometimes added up to very important clues.

When Kary and Camden came in from church, I told Kary about her next assignment, and she was all for it. She'd also heard back from Diamond.

"She left a message saying she could meet me this afternoon. Do you have any idea what she charges for a reading?"

I opened my desk drawer. "No, but the agency can advance you a hundred dollars from the emergency fund." I handed her the cash. "If she mentions a tall, dark handsome man who's an expert at solving crimes, you'll know she's legit."

She sat down in the chair I have for clients. "I've decided to call Mooresville tomorrow and see if they can give me a few more days to make a decision."

"School doesn't start until August, right? I imagine they can wait."

"Depends on how many other people want the job. We'll see. Now I need to find a scarf with a lot of fringe and a headband."

"You're meeting Diamond dressed as a hippy?"

"I want to look like someone who believes in all things supernatural."

"You are someone who believes in all things supernatural. You could go as you are."

She glanced at her Sunday dress, a light pink little number with a floral design, and wrinkled her nose. "Where's the fun in that?"

She hopped up. "I wonder if Stuart's got anything I could use."

"I think you should go as Randy Raccoon."

She grinned. "I've always wanted to try on that outfit."

She went upstairs to rifle through Stuart's collection of over-sized animal costumes, hats, and other items he used for his birthday party gigs. I wanted to do something constructive, only I wasn't sure what would be constructive at this moment. I needed a porch break.

I had just sat down in a rocking chair when Lily came through the hedge at the side of the house and up the front steps. Her fashion choice for the day was a pale yellow dress over a green-striped blouse, green clogs, and a large felt hat that looked like it once belonged to Robin Hood. She greeted me and had chosen a rocking chair when Denny's yellow Le Baron pulled in the drive. Denny hopped out, a vision—or nightmare, depending on your point of view—in a blue satin dress, matching heels, and pearls.

He took one look at Lily and shuddered. "Good heavens, what an ensemble. Doesn't that poor thing have a mother?"

"Maybe you could give her some fashion tips."

I was being flippant, but Denny took me seriously. "I'd be delighted."

I introduced them. They were instantly intrigued with each other, Lily staring up as if she were in the presence of one of her aliens, Denny smiling down as if he'd found a challenge worthy of his talents.

In addition to amusing Denny, I realized Lily could be the perfect distraction for me. "Something I can do for you, Lily?" I asked.

She came out of her trance. "Oh, yes, David. Would you mind taking me to pick up some more things from the Dimity House?

You have such a large car with all that trunk space."

"What sort of things?"

"Mr. Frost says we may have the rest of the chandelier and some stained glass windows. He's totally remodeling."

"Okay, when do you want to go?"

"Is now okay?"

"Sure."

Denny carefully lifted the hem of her dress. "Lily, dearest, if I might make just the teensiest suggestion, this color is all wrong for you."

Her eyes went wide. "But yellow is one of my primary force colors."

"It's all wrong for you. You're a Winter, dear. You should never wear pastels."

"A Winter?"

Denny sighed. "I can see we have a lot to talk about."

They settled on the porch for a fashion update. Realizing I had some time before the excursion to the Dimity House, I went in to the kitchen where Camden was cutting ham and cheese slices for sandwiches.

"Did you find out anything from Sherry's husband?" he asked.

"I haven't heard from him."

"Did Sherry ever give you that list you wanted?"

"I have an idea that list would be so long I'd never get to the end of it."

From the porch we heard Lily and Denny laughing.

"That's something new," Camden said.

"Let's see what's going on."

He put the sandwiches and a bag of chips on a tray and carried it out to the porch while I brought the drinks. We arrived in time to hear Denny say, "Now I can show you how to fix that hair. It really is the most unusual color."

He'd gotten her to take off her ridiculous hat. I'd never seen Lily without a hat. Her white hair billowed around her pretty little face like dandelion fluff. He'd also tied the sash of the dress tighter to reveal her tiny waist and rolled up the sleeves of the blouse.

"Wow, Lily, you look great," I said, and Camden agreed.

She blushed. "I told Denny I really don't care that much about my looks."

He held up his hands. "But why hide it? Flaunt it, that's my motto, flaunt it good."

They laughed together like old friends.

"Now I want you to go home and look in your closet for something in a nice rose pink or royal blue," Denny told her. "And if all your hats are like this one, you simply must throw them away."

She looked worried. "But if I look too good, the aliens might not be able to resist."

"Is that all you're worried about? Goodness me. If they abducted you looking like a sack of potatoes, they have no taste whatsoever. I say, screw the aliens. Dress any way you please."

Lily looked as if she wanted to believe him.

"Have you had lunch?" Camden asked them. "We've got plenty of sandwiches."

"Thank you," Lily said. She took one and sat down in a rocking chair.

Denny sat down in the rocking chair next to Lily's and spread several napkins on his blue satin lap before taking a sandwich.

"How's the show going?" Camden asked him.

"Well, you know there can't be a show without all sorts of

drama," he said. "As I told David earlier, several actors had jumped ship, which is why I was desperately needed. The latest defector was a perfectly fine Cable, and what does he do but go down the road to another theater to take a part in their production of *Cats*! The director is furious. We open in two weeks and we don't have a Cable."

"Call the cable company," I said.

Denny made a little exasperated sound. "David. A Lieutenant Cable. We're doing *South Pacific*. He's one of the leads. He sings 'Younger Than Springtime.' He sings 'You've Got to be Carefully Taught.' He gets to make out with a beautiful underage native girl and then he dies. Millions will weep! It's a fabulous part." He eyed Camden. "Cam, you know you'd make a perfectly darling Marine."

"No, thanks," he said. "I'm on full-time baby patrol."

"Believe me, we've searched and searched. We are desperate. We're back to square one."

"Speaking of square," I said, "isn't *South Pacific* one of those older, more traditional musicals, like *Sound of Music*? I thought the new director was more *avant garde*."

"It's a totally new concept," Denny said. "You haven't lived until you've seen our chorus of 'There is Nothing Like a Dame.'"

"Now that I'd pay money to see."

"Cam, you ought to think about it."

"Don't Marines have to be six feet tall?" I asked.

Denny waved a hand. "Piffle! Mere details."

Camden had a more pressing concern. "I'd have to cut my hair."

"No, no! This is not your typical musical production. We're taking all kinds of liberties."

I grinned. "On stage and off."

Denny rolled his eyes at me. "How did you guess, you wicked thing?"

"I know someone," Lily said.

The three of us put our sandwiches down and turned to her.

"You do?" Denny said. "Tell me more. What does he look like? Can he sing? Has he done any theater before?"

"He's a member of the ASG."

"Abductees Support Group," I explained.

Denny's mouth made a silent "O."

"He's as tall as David and he has a very nice voice," Lily said. She dug in the pocket of her dress for her phone. "I can give you his number."

"At this point, I am willing to try anyone," Denny said. He put the number in his phone. "Thank you, Lily."

"He might need a night off to meet with the group," she said, "but I think he'd enjoy the experience of being in a play."

"I wouldn't dream of interfering with his therapy." His glance to me said, what am I getting into here? "It will be an experience for everyone."

Lily looked pleased, and Camden assured Denny the ASG member was a reasonable fellow. He didn't add "And not a nutcase," but Denny took the meaning and thanked Lily again.

This weighty matter solved, I asked Denny what he knew about Sherry White's ex-husband, Mitch Stratton.

"Let me see." He counted the information off on his fingers. "Tall, dark, and handsome like you, only you're way more handsome, David."

"Thanks. Was he also an actor?"

"I believe so. Yes, but he made only one movie. *Tempting Fate?* Tempting something. I'll think of it in a minute. He and Sherry made a nice couple, but broke up after about five years."

It took just a few seconds to type "Mitch Stratton" and "Tempting" into my phone. Mitch Stratton was listed as "Vance" in *Tempting Lust*, a cheesy-looking movie that had gone straight to video. This had not been mentioned on his website, no doubt for obvious reasons.

"*Tempting Lust*," I told Denny.

"Well, why couldn't I remember that? It sounds charming."

"I'll see if I can find it and we'll have movie night."

"I can hardly wait," he said.

We finished lunch and then I asked Lily if she was ready to go. Ignoring Denny's heavy sigh, she put her hat back on. "Ready."

# CHAPTER EIGHT

*"Picture Me Dancing"*

On the drive out to the Dimity House, Lily was unusually quiet. As we chugged up the steep curving drive, she said, "David, I really like Cam's friend, but I kind of like the way I dress."

"Don't let Denny or anyone else influence you, then," I said. "Wear what you want."

When we arrived, a tall man stood at the front door. His somber face and black clothes made him look like a raven, the perfect ornament for the Dimity House, a huge gray mansion Edgar Alan Poe would have enjoyed for a summer retreat. I parked beside a moving van full of modern furniture, all wires and odd angles, and some black and white photographs in silver frames. From what I could see of the photos, they were pictures of children, children romping in the flowers, hanging upside down from trees, sitting on grandma's lap, opening presents on Christmas—all kinds of cheery precious memory things like that.

Lily hopped out and introduced me. "David, this is Jason Frost, the new owner. Jason, this is my friend, David Randall. He's a detective."

Up close, Jason Frost looked less serious. Laugh lines crinkled around his dark eyes. "No mystery here, although it sure looks like the perfect setting for one."

"It's a little gloomy," I said.

"Give me about a month. You won't recognize the place." He indicated the room behind him, which was filled with ugly dark furniture. "As soon as I can get all of Burke's stuff out of here, everything gets a paint job, beige and white. Then I'll get some skylights in, polish these floors. It'll look completely different."

I tried to imagine the dark hallway beige. "What made you decide to buy this house?"

"I'm opening a new gallery for my work. Let me show you."

He gave us a tour of the house. A large oak staircase dominated the front hallway. Dark rooms spread out in every direction, carpeted in gray and brown, the patterns faded and filled with dust. Frost pulled back dark draperies to show us the wide windows, and the effect of light in the rooms was surprisingly cheerful. In the front room, two crystal chandeliers lay in a glittering pile, and four stained glass windows rested against the wall.

"Take what you want, Miss Wilkes," Jason Frost said to Lily. "The rest goes in the trash. Please be careful, though. I cut my finger on one of the broken ones."

We helped Lily carry the windows to the car where they fit easily in the Fury's trunk. While she untangled the remaining crystals from the chandeliers, Frost gestured to several pictures propped against one wall. More angelic children's faces beamed from the photographs. "My latest series: The Joys of Summer."

Children peeked over hay bales, danced in the surf, shared ice cream cones with their dogs. "Very nice," I said.

"I don't know if you've heard of me, but I'm famous for my children's portraits," Frost said. "Perhaps you have a child, or a niece or nephew? Let me give you one of my cards. My studio's already set up. If you know of someone who'd like a nice portrait, give me a call."

"Thank you." I looked at another row of black and white photos and spied a familiar face. "Is that Sherry White?"

"Yes, when I was first starting out, I did quite a lot of celebrity portraits. I think you'll recognize all the people in this series."

Frost's picture of Sherry showed a calm woman with a wistful expression. "You've captured a whole different side of her."

"That was when she was first starting out, too. She'd just left the Marigolds for a solo career. I understand she's quite the diva these days."

"Have you been in contact with her lately?" I asked.

"Oh, no. That photo session was years ago."

"She's in town for some concerts."

"I read about that in the paper. I have to admit I never cared for her music. I'm a country music fan, myself. And you?"

"Traditional jazz."

"Ah," he said in that abstracted way people answer when they have no idea what traditional jazz is.

Lily decided she wanted the chandeliers as well as the crystals, so Frost and I carried them out to the car. One fit in the trunk. I put the other on the back seat. Lily shook Frost's hand.

"Thanks so much, Jason. We can really use the crystals."

"No problem. They're not my style." He dusted his hands. "That's it, then. Oh, my card. I almost forgot." He went back into the house and returned with a card for me and one for Lily. "I'd like to take your picture, as well, Miss Wilkes. Give me a call if you're interested."

"I think he's very nice," Lily said as we drove back down the winding driveway.

"Looks like he's got some good ideas for fixing up the place."

She turned Frost's card over in her hands. "He said he'd like to take my picture."

"Do you want your picture taken?" Maybe she thought it would give away her location to the aliens.

"I haven't had a picture made in a long time." She fingered the brim of her hat. "You know, I might want to give Denny's suggestions a try, though, just for fun. He seems to know a lot about fashion." She looked out the window. "Karl knew a lot about fashion, too."

"Who's Karl?"

"Somebody I knew before I was abducted the first time. When I came back, he didn't believe anything I said. He thought I'd run out on him. It made him mad."

I'd never heard Lily talk about her past. "I'm sorry."

"It's okay. People believe what they want to. I guess I'm better off without him. Friends are supposed to stand by you no matter what, right?"

"Right."

After a pause, she said, "Do you think Denny would be a good friend?"

"He's one of Camden's oldest friends. That's good enough for me."

When we got to Lily's house, I hauled everything up onto her front porch. She thanked me again.

"Thank you for fixing Denny's cable," I said, which made her laugh.

\*\*\*

I returned to my office and got back on the Internet. I searched for "Sherry White" and "Marigolds" and found some interesting stories.

I'd never heard of the Marigolds, but then, I never listen to the radio except for the news and sports. About ten years ago, the Marigolds had been one of the hottest girl groups around. Sherry, Tracey Page, and Patricia Lansdale always dressed in yellow. They had three top ten hits: "Love Me Every Way You Can," "Kisses By the Bunch," and their biggest hit right before Sherry left the group, "Touched By Your Heart." According to this source, when Sherry left, it was worse than Diana Ross leaving the Supremes. The group fell apart. The other women were left without careers. Tracey Page died of a drug overdose, and Patricia Lansdale moved to Tampa, Florida. After a brief internet search, I found her number.

The remaining Marigold's voicemail said, "Hello! You've reached Patricia Lansdale now performing at the Midnight Club. Please call again or leave a message."

I left a message, telling her I was a reporter for the *Parkland Herald* in North Carolina and that Sherry White was in town for a series of concerts.

"Everyone knows everything about Sherry White," I said, "but the focus of my article is going to be on the other two members of the Marigolds and what's been happening in their lives since your tragic breakup. I hope that's not too painful a subject to discuss."

I was *en route* to the kitchen for a soda when a bright red Metro zipped into our driveway and Valerie Banner got out, followed by a small scrawny man who seemed bursting with energy. I met them on the porch.

"Before you say anything, let me explain why I'm here," Valerie said. "I want you to meet my Uncle Jake."

Jake Banner was a live wire of a man from his electric blue eyes to thousand-volt grin, two things he shared with his niece. He had on a jarring combination of blue slacks and a lime green shirt printed with pink flamingoes. His handshake, like all his movements, was quick and decisive.

"Got your message, Randall. Bigfoot sighting, eh? Nice one. You solved Taft Finch's murder, right? He was a pal of mine. Nice work."

"Thanks," I said.

"What's Val been bugging you about?"

"She's looking for the Big Story."

"Aren't we all, pal, aren't we all?" He stuck his hands in his pockets and rocked on his heels. "This friend of yours wouldn't be the same Camden whose wife runs the PSN?"

"That's the one."

His grin broadened. "Had a chat with her once. Once was enough. He's the genuine article, though. Ought to be making a fortune, but what's he doing instead? Tryin' to make it go away."

"It's his choice."

"Hey, I don't blame him. My partner's the same way. Got a real affinity for the paranormal, but he won't admit it. I just follow him along and interview whatever he attracts. Been some great stuff, too. Vampires, ghosts. He always finds some explanation that makes him happy. Me, I know better. Anyway, the reason I'm here is to tell you Val's harmless. She just wants a story."

"Will she do anything to get one?" I asked.

"Hey," she said, offended. "I'm right here."

Jake kept grinning. "She might. She's been following my career since she was five, and I've set a brilliant example: climbing trees, walls, going through trashcans, bribing waiters and maids and doormen, dressing up like a bag lady—the usual tabloid news gathering techniques."

"How about breaking and entering? Blackmail?"

This brought another sputter of protest from Valerie.

"Maybe a little trespassing, but no, nothing that serious," her uncle said. "You have read the *Galaxy*, haven't you? We don't have to put ourselves in real danger to find out Elvis made a farewell appearance on the *Titanic*."

"What about Tony Kenner?" I asked.

Jake Banner made a face. "He's pretty low even for the 'bloids."

"Has he got something on Sherry White? He won't answer his phone."

"I don't know. Stop by the office sometime and we'll find out."

"I'll do that, thanks."

He checked his watch. "Let's haul it, Val. I gotta be in the Bermuda Triangle by six."

"Okay," Valerie said. "You see, David? I'm not what you think I am."

I didn't know why she cared what I thought, but if dragging her colorful uncle by to say hello made her feel better, that was okay by me. If he knew something useful about Tony Kenner, then I definitely wasn't going to argue.

"Okay," I said. "Have a nice trip, Mr. Banner."

"Call me Jake." He got in the car and gave a friendly wave. Valerie gave me a long stare I couldn't interpret.

"There's a story here, David, and I'm going to find it."

"Go for it."

She hopped in the Metro and drove away.

# CHAPTER NINE

### *"Reflection Dance"*

As I went back inside, Camden came down the stairs carrying Elise. He'd found it easiest to catch some sleep during the day when the baby slept. Elise slept and ate all day and all night, so we didn't hear her little voice very often.

I followed him into the kitchen and held Elise while he retrieved another bottle from the fridge to warm up in the microwave. Her favorite toy, a rainbow fabric ball, was on the counter next to the ceramic grocery frog that held all our extra change. I was reaching for it when it rolled away from me. Elise made a little gurgling sound. I glanced at the baby in time to see her opening and closing her little fist. The ball rolled back and forth.

"Uh, Camden."

He turned from the microwave. Elise spread her hand wide, and the ball stopped.

She continued her grasping motion until the ball moved to the edge of the counter where it fell off. Her little face scrunched up, ready to cry.

Camden picked up the ball. "It's okay, Elise. Here you go." His expression was a mixture of pride and concern. He patted her head as she chewed happily on her prize. "Good job."

"Good lord, you mean," I said. "Go ahead and check telekinesis off the list."

"I knew she could," he said. "But I didn't expect it this soon."

He finished warming her bottle and I handed her over. I checked my watch. Almost five. A little early for supper, but watching Elise chug her milk made me realize I was hungry. "How about a snack? I could go for a hot dog or two, and maybe Elise can make them fly."

"That sounds good. But not flying hot dogs."

My phone rang. It was Kary checking in from her meeting with Diamond.

"Mission accomplished," she said.

"Come join us at Janice's," I said. "Preferably not as Randy Raccoon."

"Oh, that outfit was way too hot. Here's what Katarina Klomsky wore to her reading."

In a few moments, a selfie popped onto my phone. Kary had hidden her hair in an elaborate scarf, draped a fringed shawl around her shoulders, and put on a pair of large dark-framed glasses.

"Ms. Klomsky, you look like that addled Divination teacher from *Harry Potter*," I said. "Could I please have Kary back?"

"Show Cam how I look."

I turned the phone so Camden could comment. "Very retro, Katarina."

"I'm on my way."

\*\*\*

In a short while, the real Kary met us at Janice Chan's hot dog restaurant. We sat outside at one of the picnic tables to enjoy hot dogs fixed all the way, crispy French fries, and sodas. Camden had brought along a second bottle for Elise, and she was working her way through it.

"Look at her go," Kary said.

"She worked up an appetite trying out her telekinesis," he said.

"What? Really? That's amazing."

He put her over his shoulder and patted her back until she burped. Her little hands reached for the bottle. "Amazing and frightening all in one."

"What did she do?"

"Tried to get her rainbow ball to come to her. She almost got it."

"Well, my report is not going to be amazing or frightening." She licked ketchup off her fingers. "Here's what Diamond told me. She said I was an old soul searching for meaning, a believer and a dreamer who loved all things unseen and was open to the more fanciful realms of reality."

"Your disguise worked, then," I said.

"Perfectly. She said I would have a wonderful relationship with a red-haired man."

"So she picked up on Rufus. Yes, go on."

"That my family was large and supportive."

"Off the tracks there."

"And I would own not one but two pieces of property, one of which would become a wildlife refuge."

"She's taking over 302 Grace, Camden. Wildlife refuge is not a bad description."

Elise had finished her second bottle and seemed full for the moment. Camden shifted her to his other arm so he could reach his hot dog. "In light of Elise's new talent, I agree."

Kary paused to take a drink of soda. "After my reading, I mentioned I'd heard she worked for Sherry White and what was that like? Boy, did she let me know what it was like. You can check my ears for scorch marks. I said I'd heard about the threatening letters, and Diamond informed me those letters were no less than what Sherry deserved, that her past was coming back to haunt her. She didn't get specific, and by then, my time was up. Sorry I didn't learn anything more helpful."

"We learned Diamond's not psychic," I said. "But I sort of knew that."

"That's true. She charged me sixty dollars, by the way, so here's your change."

As she dug in her pocketbook for the money, I said, "Keep it. You might need it for the spa."

"I hope I have better luck there." She poked a French fry into the little paper cup of ketchup. "What have you guys been doing?"

"I took Lily to pick up chandelier crystals at the Dimity House and met the new owner, Jason Frost," I said. "He's a photographer, and he had a photo of Sherry, so there's another connection to investigate."

"I believe Katarina Klomsky would like to have her picture made."

"Excellent idea. And I just happen to have his card. As for my internet searching, I hoped to find two vengeful ex-Marigolds, but one died of a drug overdose, and the other one, Patricia Lansdale, has her own nightclub act."

"So it's possible Patricia has forgiven Sherry for leaving them?"

Kary asked.

"Yes, oh, and Valerie brought her Uncle Jake by the house. He agreed with me that Tony Kenner is slime. As soon as Jake gets back from the Bermuda Triangle, we'll check in at the *Galaxy* office and have a word with Kenner if he's there."

Kary juggled her hot dog so the onions stayed in place. "So what's next?"

"Denny mentioned that Sherry's ex-husband was in a movie called *Tempting Lust.* Camden and I have an overwhelming desire to see this cinematic prize."

"Ooo, sounds spicy."

"We thought we'd give Movie World a try."

\*\*\*

To our surprise, Movie World had a DVD of *Tempting Lust,* so we settled in the island with some drinks and popcorn and fast-forwarded until we found Vance, Mitch Stratton's character. The movie was dated and full of clichés, your basic soap opera of adultery and coveting and jealousy. I understood completely why *Tempting Lust* wasn't on anyone's top ten list. However, Stratton wasn't a bad actor. If he'd been in a movie with a better script and better production values, he might have made it in Hollywood. The movie was listed as a Crystal Films Production. The copyright date on the box corresponded with the year he was married to Sherry.

"Think he used his status as Mr. Sherry White to land a movie role?" I asked. "Or maybe being married to her was a liability. Maybe nobody wanted to work with him because she came attached."

Camden set his large plastic cup of Coke on the coffee table. "He might have been a struggling actor before he met Sherry."

"Maybe he decided he'd rather direct. Most of them do." I checked my email, but there was no reply from Images, Stratton's company.

After another twenty minutes we decided our lust had been tempted enough, but just before I stopped the movie, the picture went blank.

"Uh, oh," I said. "This is what happens when you lust too much."

"Must be a glitch in the DVD," Kary said. "It's pretty old."

"Or some scenes were cut."

The blank space lasted a few minutes and then the movie resumed.

"Well, we'll never know," I said. "Unless we find another copy that's complete. A problem for another day."

Camden had watched the blank space, his expression puzzled.

"Can you see what's missing?" I asked.

"Just darkness."

"Uh, oh," I said again. "Serious darkness? Evil spirit darkness?"

"It's hard to tell," he said. "Maybe it has something to do with a missing scene."

"I'll find out right now," Kary said.

Camden took Elise upstairs to bed. Kary and I moved to the sofa where she opened her laptop and looked up Crystal Films. The company was very small with only five films produced, including *Tempting Promises* and *Tempting Shadows*. Neither film listed Mitch Stratton in the credits. None of the other movies did, either. We checked all the dates. Crystal Films hadn't put out a new movie in ten years. As for *Tempting Lust*, there was no mention of any missing scenes, or a director's cut, or any problems with censors that would cause a blank spot in the movie.

"Doesn't look like much of a lead, does it?" Kary said.

"No, but there may be more to this story. I'll try to contact him again tomorrow."

She closed the laptop. "Well, Katarina will discover all kinds of leads when she goes to Jason Frost's."

"If he isn't too overcome by your amazing style."

"It is amazing, isn't it? I think it's my favorite disguise so far." Then she gave me a worried look. "You don't suppose there's anything to this darkness Cam saw in the movie, I mean, like the serious darkness we had to deal with before?"

I didn't want to deal with any kind of darkness. "We'll just have to hope we got a rough copy of *Tempting Lust*," I said.

# CHAPTER TEN

## *"Too Hurt to Dance"*

That night I dreamed a whole row of Sherry White's ex-husbands lined up next to a whole row of Sherrys and started screaming at each other. I went down the line, trying to get them to shut up. At the very end of the line stood Camden and Ellin, arguing just as loudly.

"Where's Elise?" I asked them, but they wouldn't stop. I was getting panicked when Kary came up to me and said, "The train's here."

"What train?" I said. "I don't want to go anywhere."

"We have to," she said.

I heard the chugging sound of an approaching locomotive. A train? What was a train doing here? I didn't want to get on a train. Where were we going? Was I going to have to ride with all the Bickersons?

I was awakened by the sound of the washing machine chugging away downstairs. For a moment, I expected to hear the toot-toot of a train whistle. Kary's side of the bed was empty, and I remembered she was infiltrating the Healing Day Spa this morning. I yawned and stretched and looked at the clock. Almost nine-thirty. Damn crazy dreams.

I staggered up and got dressed. I went down the stairs to the laundry room to toss yesterday's dirty clothes in with the load. Camden was taking a pile of clothes out of the dryer.

"What's in the wash?" I asked.

"Miscellaneous stuff. Yours can go in."

I lifted the lid and tossed in my laundry. As Camden began to fold Elise's little onesies, I felt a strange sense of panic. "Where's Elise?"

"She's staying with Ellie's mom today."

Okay. Leftover dream anxiety. "Man, I didn't mean to sleep so late."

"You need pizza."

Fortunately, because their service is famously slow, Pokey's Pizza opens at ten. We ordered the More Meat Than You Need extravaganza. When it finally arrived, we ate on the porch. Our housecat Cindy and her black and white kitten Oreo, now a healthy eight pounds, slithered around hopefully underneath my rocking chair and the porch swing. I had a Coke, and Camden had his usual sugar-laden iced tea.

"So what's next?" he asked.

I peeled another slice of pizza from the box, dislodging hunks of hamburger and sausage that fell and were immediately pounced upon by Cindy and Oreo. "I hope to get an email from that old lust tempter, Vance, aka Mitch Stratton, today. I haven't heard back from Patricia Lansdale, either, or Tony Kenner."

We ate in silence for a while, watching the birds scrabble for seeds at the feeder. A neighbor drove by, honked his horn in greeting, and we waved.

Camden set his cup aside. "Ellie's been pestering me again about looking at houses. Do you think I'm being unreasonable about not wanting to move?"

Ellin had yet to give up on her dream of living in a swankier neighborhood. "Hell, no. This is your home."

"I don't think she's ever going to warm up to the place."

"She grew up in a mansion, remember? Plus you have a psychic connection she can't access. Have you told her about Elizabeth?" Elizabeth Singer was the original owner and guardian spirit of 302 Grace. I'd have laughed this off as one of Camden's more bizarre visions except that I'd seen her, too. She was very attractive for a woman who's been dead since 1935.

"Yes, she knows about her."

"Do you tell Ellin everything?"

"Pretty much."

"Even about Tamara?"

He paused. He'd had a pretty steamy relationship with his boss before his engagement to Ellin. "Well, not all the details. We've talked about Tamara. Ellie's okay with that."

"How about Michelle? Is she okay with that?"

"That was years ago."

"I seem to recall a Catherine, too, and wasn't there one with a fairy tale name? Not Snow White. Rose Redd, that's it, the redhead who—"

"Don't you have email to check on?"

I grinned and took out my phone. There was a reply from Images, thanking me for my interest and listing a phone number.

Stratton's voice was low and pleasant. "Mr. Randall, so glad you called. I certainly appreciate your generous offer, but fortunately, 'Rice Farmers in Crisis' has been fully funded. You did see that the company is closing?"

"Yes, and I'm sorry to hear that," I said. "There was something else I wanted to discuss with you. I've gotten permission from Sherry White to film a day in the life of a famous singer," I said. "I'd planned to hire you."

Mitch Stratton cleared his throat. "Mr. Randall, are you aware I was once married to Sherry White, and we parted on less than amiable terms?"

I let myself wait a brief shocked moment. "Sorry. I had no idea."

"It's quite all right. I'm sure she never mentions my name. But you see the problem."

"She didn't say a word to me about your former relationship. She just said, get the best photographer."

"I'm flattered, but I'm not really a photographer," he said. "I'm what you'd call a visual designer. I create the concept for my films and then try to interpret that concept through them. Even if Images was still in business, the minute she found out my company was doing a film about her she'd refuse to have anything to do with it."

"I understand," I said, "but this has all the makings of a block-buster. Poor girl makes good, top ten records, death threats."

His tone changed. "Death threats? What are you talking about?"

"Sherry White has received several very graphic threatening letters. The police haven't been able to find the writer. You see the built-in drama here?"

But Mitch Stratton didn't react as a film-maker who senses a juicy story. "Is she all right? Does she have protection?" He sounded genuinely concerned.

"Oh, yes, bodyguards all over the place. She's still very nervous, though."

"It doesn't take much to get her excited," he said. "I'm very sorry to hear that, Mr. Randall, but, as you'll see if you spend much time with her, she's not an easy person to get along with. I'm afraid she's made a lot of enemies, although I don't know anyone who'd go so far as to actually hurt her. You said the police were on the case?"

"Yes, and she's hired a private investigator."

"That's good to know. She should be all right, then."

I wanted to hear Stratton's side of the story. "How long were you married, if you don't mind me asking?"

"Five years. It all started very nicely, but as she became more and more famous, she wanted less and less to do with me. I had what I thought were some good ideas for her production company, but she's the kind of woman that if it isn't her own idea, she's not interested."

"I've seen some of Miss White's movies," I said.

"Oh, none of those were mine. Sherry prefers the big screen epics. I kept telling her she could have real success with smaller films, the kind that really delve into character."

Like *Tempting Lust?* I wanted to ask.

"But she wasn't interested, so I left to start Images," he said. "I really would've liked to have been a part of her life, but when two people want to be in control of the same thing, somebody's got to give."

"Are you an actor, also, Mr. Stratton?"

"I toyed with the idea, but acting just wasn't for me."

I wondered if that had been his decision.

"As for Sherry's current trouble, I've been in Beijing for about six months now, so I'm way out of the loop. I'm heading back to Virginia this week to visit my family, but I doubt she'd want to hear from me."

"Well, thanks for your time," I said. "I'm sorry this didn't work out, but I'll keep you in mind for future projects."

"Thanks," he said, "and thanks for the news about Sherry. I'd appreciate it if you'd keep me informed about her situation. You have my number."

I told him I'd be glad to and ended the call. There was one more piece of pizza, so I took it. "Stratton sounds like he cares. He also says he was never interested in acting. Maybe the experience of *Tempting Lust* was too traumatic."

"Speaking of acting, I promised Denny I'd come to his rehearsal. Can you give me a ride to the theater this evening?" Camden said. "Denny said I wouldn't have to stay for the whole thing."

"I happen to be available. If Denny knows all about Sherry White, I'll bet some of the actors do, too."

I tried Patricia Lansdale's number and again got her voicemail. I spent more time on the Internet, searching for more information about Mitch Stratton. When I went back to www.images.com, a message popped up saying "no site found," so what he'd told me was true. Images had folded.

Just like Crystal Films?

As for my other suspect, Tony Kenner's phone continued to buzz with a busy signal.

"Right now I have this overwhelming urge to call the PSN," I said to Camden. "What's my problem?"

"Your aura's out of alignment."

"Excellent." I punched in Ellin's number. When she answered, I said, "I need some advice. I feel my aura is fluctuating."

"Randall," she said with a growl. "I'll fluctuate your aura for you."

"Did Diamond come in for her interview?" I asked.

"Yes, and I told her we had a part-time position with our help line available if she was interested. She seemed not only interested but relieved. I hired her."

"Great. Can you keep an eye on her? See if she does anything unusual?"

"That will not be a problem," Ellin said. "I always keep an eye on my new employees. Am I looking for anything in particular?"

"If she starts scribbling death threats in big black letters on yellow paper, give me a call."

I thought Ellin would fuss at me for wasting her time and hang up, but she surprised me. "All right," she said and ended the call.

"If I didn't know better, I'd say Ellin enjoys playing detective almost as much as Kary," I said. "We should be hearing from her by now, shouldn't we?"

"Text on the way," Camden said.

My phone chimed its incoming text sound. From Kary, of course. Her text read, "On my way home with big news."

When Kary arrived, she was beaming, and not just from a morning at Healing Day Spa. She was too excited to sit down.

"David, you told me the seminar was full and Sherry was insisting on privacy, so I had an idea. I signed up for another seminar called Calming Soul that was at the same time as Soothing Waters. I thought I might be able to slip into Sherry's seminar, you know, the way I used to sneak into different theaters at the movies. Then I'd say, 'Oops, I'm sorry. All these doors look alike.'"

"Another example of your corrupt childhood," I said.

"Exactly. First I went to the Calming Soul seminar," she said.

"I sat near the back, and when there was a break, I wandered down the hall to the main room where I knew the Soothing Waters seminar was being held. Soothing Waters was on break, too, so I started chatting with some of the participants as we all walked to the ladies room. They told me yes, Sherry White was taking part, but she was sitting by herself in a private room off the main meeting room. Well, I'd taken the time to familiarize myself with the layout of Healing Day Spa, and I knew there were little meditation chambers, as they called them, in a circle around a big fountain. You could access them through the main room, or you could go around through the Peace Garden past the labyrinth."

"A labyrinth?" I said. "Isn't that too spooky for a Peace Garden?"

"It's not the kind guarded by a Minotaur. It's flat stones arranged in a pattern that's supposed to help you focus. Anyway, I walked around it a couple of times in case anyone was watching, and then sidled over to the glass doors that opened to the fountain, slipped inside, and sat down as if I were meditating by the fountain. I didn't know which little chamber was Sherry's, but as it turned out, I didn't have to guess. I could hear her."

"Screeching for peace and quiet?"

"Talking to herself. She started with something that sounded like a mantra, and then she was crying. I heard her say, 'This isn't working. I don't know why I even tried.' I thought she was by herself, but another voice answered her."

"One of her other personalities?"

"No, this was a man's voice. He must have been one of the seminar leaders. He said, 'You're too hard on yourself. You can relax if you let go of all this negative energy,' and Sherry said, 'It's too late. I thought you could help me, but this is a waste of time. I should never have done this.' The man suggested some other mantras, but she wasn't interested. She told him to leave. That's when I almost got caught."

"What happened?" Camden asked.

"I didn't have time to hide. The man came out of the chamber in a hurry, as if he couldn't get away from Sherry fast enough. He said, 'Oh, can I help you?' in that tone that means, 'What the hell are you doing here?' I apologized and said I'd been in one of the chambers yesterday and lost an earring and had hoped it was still on the floor. He became real nice and helpful then. 'Let me see if it's in our lost and found,' he said. 'This way, please.'"

"Very slick," I said.

"Thanks. I said I didn't mean to pry, but thought I heard Sherry White's voice. When I assured him I wasn't stalking her or trying to disturb her meditation, he said yes, it was her. I remembered what Cam said about Sherry's stage fright, so I said, 'Oh, is she getting help with her stage fright? I often have that, too.' 'I knew you had to be an actress,' he said." She made a face indicating she'd heard this line before and continued. "We didn't find my earring, of course, but I thanked him and apologized again for interrupting his session with Sherry. He said, 'Oh, that was over.' Then he said the spa was especially beautiful and calming at night and if I decided to come back, he'd be happy to give me a private tour."

"Gosh, how nice of him," I said.

She grinned. "I said I'd think about it."

"When Sherry said, 'This isn't working. I don't know why I even tried,' she must have been talking about the seminar," Camden said, "but then she said, 'It's too late.' I wonder what she meant by that? 'It's too late' sounds drastic for a meditation technique."

Kary shrugged. "We all know Sherry tends to be overdramatic."

"Still, excellent work," I said. "Any word from Mooresville?"

She checked her wrist watch. "They said they'd let me know today, but I haven't heard anything yet. Guess I'll have to wait. I should get ready for my piano students. I have two coming this afternoon." Her expression changed. "Damn, I forgot about my students! If I move to Mooresville, I'll have to give them up, and some of them are doing so well."

"*If* you move to Mooresville," I said. "That means it's not a done deal."

# CHAPTER ELEVEN

*"Dancing in the Dark"*

That evening, I took Camden to the Parkland Little Theater. As we walked into the pearl gray auditorium, voices called from above the stage, and colors splashed on the backdrop as the technicians adjusted the lights. Down in the orchestra pit, someone played the piano and someone else tuned a clarinet. Camden and I could immediately tell this production of *South Pacific* was going to be different. The little bits of the movie I'd seen on TV involved a beach, some sailors, and an old native woman singing about an island called Bali Ha'i. This set was a lush forest, all pink and purple, with silver palm trees. A few sailors in traffic cone orange stood around talking to hunky native boys in shiny green grass loincloths.

The director came down the aisle to greet us. He was a tall dark man with windswept hair, narrow critical eyes, and one of those little pencil line mustaches. "Good evening, gentlemen. Welcome. I'm Jubal Whitley. You must be David Randall, and I recognize Camden from his performance in *My Fair Lady*. It's a shame you aren't available to do this show, Cam, but fortunately, Denny found a young man who's going to work out very well for our Cable."

"This is quite a set," I said. "And really bright costumes."

"Some of the cast like to rehearse in costume," Whitley said. "It helps them get into character." He spread his hands wide as he described his vision for me. "I see this as Nellie's Fever Dream. She imagines an island where men aren't afraid to show their true emotions. Here, she gets in touch with her masculine side."

This being represented by sailors in lurid orange? Camden and I exchanged a glance.

"We discover Emile de Becque is really her father, a father who always wanted a son. Nellie runs off and joins the Navy to prove herself, and finds her true purpose in life, thanks to wise advice from Bloody Mary—who's Bloody Harry in this show, by the way."

Denny waved from the stage. "That's me!" His costume consisted of a bright red shirt and a grass skirt of luminous blue and silver streamers. His hair was skinned back and wound in a top knot decorated with feathers.

Whitley continued with his vision. "Then there's the tragic B story of Lieutenant Cable and Liat. Of course he can't marry her. He and de Becque have an Understanding. But we kill him off, anyway. Then the underlying implications of 'Honey Bun' and 'You've Got to Be Carefully Taught' become amazingly clear. And before any concerned citizen goes screaming to the press about Liat being too young, my niece is playing the part. She's twenty-one."

The niece waved from her seat in the front row of the auditorium where she was taking notes for the director and cueing the actors. She had on a silky white blouse and shiny black pants. I recognized her as a member of the Slotted Spoons, aka the Destitute Dolls, a girl band I'd assisted in a previous case. Instead of her usual Goth pallor, her face was painted a warm golden shade and her dark eyes were outlined in black and silver.

"Now Cable's uniform is a touch brighter than regulation," Whitley said. "We have to underscore his neutrality in this highly charged situation. Please, have a seat. We're getting ready to run 'Younger Than Springtime.'" He motioned to his niece to come onstage. "The boys are going to do an interpretive dance behind the actors." He nodded to the man at the piano. "Take it from the intro."

I wish I could describe the interpretive dance. Lily's fellow ASG member was a tall dark-haired young man who had a good singing voice and looked completely at ease on stage. The niece was doing something I'd never seen her do, which was smile, but the real show was the chorus boys' overly dramatic posing, combined with belly dance moves. I wasn't sure this was something the good people of Parkland would understand, but at the same time, it was funny as hell.

When they'd finished, Whitley turned to me. "Well, what do you think?"

"I've never seen anything quite like it," Camden said tactfully.

"It's different," I said. "I'm not sure it's going to win you many fans."

He made a dismissive gesture. "Pooh. What do I care for public opinion? Art is Everything. All right, everyone, take five."

The chorus boys came up to make a fuss over Camden..

"So happy to see you again," one said. "I was in *My Fair Lady*. Most of us were. When are you going to try out for another?"

"I have a baby girl now," he said. "Maybe when she's older."

"A baby girl! You must bring her with you next time."

"Are you doing something for the PSN?" another asked.

"No, but I'm helping Sherry White with her stage fright," he said.

They went into orbit. "Sherry White!"

"I love her!"

"She's wonderful!"

"How did you manage that? Do you know her?"

"Randall's part of the security team," Camden said.

They made all sorts of admiring noises.

"What do you know about her?" I asked them.

"Besides the fact that she sings the most wonderful songs, we love a comeback story," one said.

"A comeback?"

This brought on another round of remarks.

"Well, Sherry's certainly not as popular as she used to be."

"She still looks fabulous, though, don't you think?"

"She never should have left the Marigolds."

"Oh, that's so true! She did her best work with them."

This prompted them to break into "Touched By Your Heart." I had to wait until they finished the chorus to ask my next question. "Is this concert tour supposed to be a comeback for Sherry?"

They looked at each other for confirmation and then nodded.

"I'd definitely say so," one said. "She hasn't done a tour this big in a while."

"I say all this publicity about those threatening letters can't hurt a bit," another said. "Even bad publicity is better than no publicity."

One leaned in to whisper. "That's why we're not worried about this show."

"All right, everyone," Whitley called. "Places for the opening number, please."

"Guys, before you go, who do you think would send threatening letters to Sherry?" I asked.

I'd hoped for some new lead, but all they came up with were the same suspects.

"The other Marigolds maybe?"

"Her ex?"

"Or one of her backup singers."

"Places!"

As the chorus scurried back on stage, Camden and I walked back up the aisle.

"Interesting that this concert tour is a comeback tour," I said. "I never realized Sherry White went away."

"So that's why she's been so frantic," he said. "These concerts are more important than usual."

"I'm sure the letter writer knows this, too."

We hadn't gone two steps before Camden stopped and turned his head as if he'd heard something.

"Do you hear that?"

"What?"

"That music."

All I could hear was the chorus working their way through "There is Nothing Like a Dame," the sound of hammers and drills, and a loud voice calling out dance steps.

Camden went back up the aisle to the steps that led backstage. "It's coming from the ballroom."

There were several rooms backstage, including dressing rooms, a prop room, and rooms for storage. The ballroom was a vast echoing room that spread out as far as we could see into the darkness, bare and still, with a dark, dusty wooden floor. I peered up into the shadows, seeing the tall windows boarded up and traces of elaborate molding along the edges of the high ceiling. The draperies were thick with dust, and the ancient chandeliers, shrouded in cobwebs, looked like huge dandelions gone to seed.

"Must have been something in its day."

Camden stepped in. "You don't hear the music?"

"Nope, sorry."

He stood very still. "Then I don't suppose you see the girl, either?"

I felt a chill down my back.

"She's coming this way. She's very indistinct, but I can tell she's young and dressed in a ball gown."

I still didn't see anything. Camden's eyes were riveted on a spot just in front of us. "What does she want?" There was an annoyingly long pause. "Camden?"

He held out his hands as if taking someone in his arms. "She wants to dance."

*All she ever wanted to do was dance.*

"Camden, this must be the spirit Lindsey wants us to help."

Apparently whatever he was seeing had a good hold, because he began to move around the ballroom as if dancing with a real woman. This went on long enough to start getting really spooky when he came to an abrupt halt.

"She's gone," he said.

"Okay," I said, "what's the deal with our phantom ballerina? You think she's a vengeful spirit? Should the guys pack up their sequins and get out of town?"

"I couldn't see her very well. As far as I could tell, she just wanted to dance."

"She wasn't here when you did *My Fair Lady*, was she?"

"No, I'm sure I would've sensed her." Camden's gaze searched the cavernous space, looking for the ghost, looking for an answer. "Didn't you say the place she was haunting was going to be destroyed? As far as I know, the theater's not scheduled for demolition."

"We'd better find out," I said.

\*\*\*

Jubal Whitley was able to confirm that yes, the ballroom needed major repairs and the city was debating whether or not it was worth saving. I said the Parkland Historical Society should get involved, and he agreed.

"I believe they are planning a fundraiser, but it may take more than they can afford."

"That solves part of the mystery," I told Camden as we walked back to my car. "According to Lindsey, if the dancer's ballroom is destroyed, she can't cross over. Now all we have to do is find however many millions of dollars it'll take to renovate the place."

"But doesn't this have to do with the dancer's music?" he asked. "If we figure out what her music is, maybe she'll be able to leave."

"You heard the music. What was it?"

"It sounded like ragtime."

"Something by Joplin, maybe?"

"Maybe," he said. "That's your area of expertise. I didn't recognize it. If we can find out who she is and what happened to her, maybe she's looking for something she lost, or wants to get a message to someone."

We both looked back at the Little Theater. "Something tells me that's going to involve a lot more dancing," I said.

# CHAPTER TWELVE

*"Dancin' 'Round and 'Round"*

T he next morning, I got up at a more reasonable hour. Kary had decided to talk to the people in Mooresville in person, so she'd already left. Camden said Ellin had decided it was Take Your Daughter to Work Day and had carried Elise off with her. I suggested to Camden this might be a good morning to check with the PSN sponsors.

The two main sponsors included Kitty Kare Kat Food and Lunch in Can. Definitely useful products you couldn't live without. We decided to start with The Merry Menagerie, the pet store that made and distributed Kitty Kare. I found the Oakland Shopping Center and parked in front of the store. When we entered, a chorus of cheeps and whistles greeted us. One side of the shop was lined with small cages filled with a variety of animals, from fat hamsters to skinny lizards. The other side held an array of pet needs: collars, bottles, dishes, aquarium rocks, and flea spray.

"Hello," a voice said from somewhere in the back. A round little woman appeared wearing a smock that said, "Paws and Give Thanks for Your Cat." "How may I help you? Oh, Mr. Camden, how nice to see you. You probably don't know me. I'm Betsy Parminter. I've met your lovely wife several times, and she's told me all about you."

Camden shook her hand and introduced me.

She cocked her head like a parakeet. "Are you a psychic also, Mr. Randall?"

"No, I'm a private investigator."

Betsy Parminter gasped. "You're a detective? Oh, this is wonderful! My two babies solve crimes all the time, just like in all the books."

"Your babies?"

She turned and called, "Tip Tip! Weener! Come to Mama."

Two large cats peered around the corner. One was orange with white feet and a white-tipped tail. The other was gray with yellow eyes and looked as if it had been riding in the dryer most of its life. Betsy scooped them up.

"This is Tip Tip," she said, indicating the orange and white cat, "and the gray one is Weener. They are absolutely brilliant at finding clues. I lost an entire carton of birdseed, and all I had to do was show them a handful, and they led me right to it, and the other day, I knew I had a special rhinestone collar for Mrs. Clarke's dog, Dribbles, and I simply could not find it, but Weener knew right where it was. He put his little paws up on my leg as if to say, 'It fell behind the counter.' When I went to see, there was Tip Tip, playing with it!"

I didn't dare look at Camden.

"You can ask them anything you want. They are such clever babies."

I thought about asking Tip Tip and Weener how many lives they had left with Betsy, but Camden, no doubt sensing my remark, spoke up.

"Mrs. Parminter, I'm sure your cats are remarkable, but we came to ask you about your sponsorship of the PSN," he said. I was amazed by how steady his voice was.

"Well, dear, I'm still a proud sponsor of the PSN. Ever since a lovely psychic woman told me about Tip Tip's Egyptian soul, I have been such a fan."

"So they can still count on your support?"

"Why, of course. Let me prove how smart my babies are!" She set the cats down. "Tip Tip, go find my checkbook." She lowered her voice to speak to me. "I know I put it down somewhere in the shop, but I just haven't been able to locate it."

Tip Tip gave me one of those disdainful looks cats have perfected over the centuries. Then she sat down, put her hind leg way up in the cello-playing position, and began to lick her underpinnings. Weener curled his lip and slouched off under the nearest counter. Betsy Parminter clasped her hands together and beamed as if her pets had just done a series of complicated back flips.

"Aren't they something?"

Tip Tip gave Camden a long stare, then sniffed and slowly wandered out. We waited politely for the cats to dash back in with the checkbook. When this didn't happen, Betsy Parminter smiled and gave us a tour of the shop.

"Sometimes it takes a while," she said.

"They're probably balancing it for you," I said, sotto voce. Camden choked on a laugh.

"We really need to go," he said, after we'd seen every fish and rat in the place and Tip Tip and Weener had yet to return, waving the missing item in triumph. "I'm sure your pets will find your checkbook for you. Thanks for your time."

"Please give my best to Ellin, and Mr. Randall, if you are ever stuck on a really hard case, please feel free to use my babies. I'd be ever so delighted."

"I'll keep that in mind, thank you," I said.

"Then after they solve the case, you could write a book and be famous."

"Certainly one of my goals in life."

We managed to wait until we were in the car before exploding with laughter.

I finally got control of myself. "So what do you think, Tip Tip?"

"I don't know, Weener. Thought I'd leave that to you."

"I know that cat told you something."

"I can't repeat it."

"At least we know she's still willing to sponsor the network." I put the Fury in gear. "Are you ready for Lunch in a Can?"

"I am always ready for Lunch in a Can."

The offices for Lunch in a Can were located in a building owned by Ultra Process, which told me everything I wanted to know right there. The receptionist was very helpful. The big boss was in a meeting, but we could speak with the second in command if we'd care to wait a few minutes.

We sat down in the outer office, a large waiting room decorated in lunch-like colors: baloney pink and peanut butter brown. On the walls were posters declaring the wonder and delight of Lunch in a Can, full color photos of the shiny cans with their aerosol buttons spraying delicious meals onto crackers, bread, and dinner plates.

"I am so hungry," I said.

"Bet we get free samples," Camden said.

"Have you ever actually eaten any of it?"

"The folks at the PSN say it has a somewhat Spam-like bouquet."

A tall, intense young woman came out of the office, told us she was glad to meet us, and assured us in all seriousness that Lunch in a Can was a proud sponsor of the PSN and would continue to be associated with such a fine program. She did, however, hope that the network could go national and expose more people to their revolutionary product. I thought perhaps this woman had sniffed one too many Lunches in Cans, but we thanked her and went on our way. As Camden had predicted, we were given free samples of the latest flavor, Sunday Picnic. We tossed the cans in the back seat.

"For our next road trip," I said.

Camden's phone rang. "Uh, oh. It's Sherry." He answered and listened, wincing. "Yes, of course. We can come over now." He looked at me, and I nodded. "Okay. Yes, you're welcome." He ended the call. "She's upset."

"Really?" I said. "How unusual."

\*\*\*

Camden and I heard Sherry's shrieks before we reached the stage.

"Did I ask for yellow? Do I *ever* want anything yellow? Yellow makes me look sallow and old! Get this out of here. Burn it."

The offending yellow thing was a piece of scenery, a nice fake brick arch with white roses. The man in charge of lighting the stage foolishly thought he'd explain.

"But, Miss White, when the light hits it, it's a beautiful cream color that compliments your hair magnificently."

Sherry White turned on him. "Are you insane? Are you listening to me? No yellow! I refuse to have that color anywhere near me."

The rest of the crew, her band, and her backup singers stood very still, as if afraid to call her wrath down upon them. I like to use calendars with "Learn a New Word Every Day" to keep in fighting shape for the vocabulary challenges we enjoy at home. A word I never thought I'd use was "virago." Looks like I was wrong.

Sherry White screamed until the piece of scenery was taken away. Then she swung around to her band. "We'll start with 'Beautiful Nights.' And get the tempo right this time."

She sang through the number six times until she was finally satisfied. She swept back her unruly hair and caught sight of us in row one. I was in mid-yawn.

"Am I boring you, Randall?"

"Not at all. Looks like you've got everything under control."

"This concert is a shambles! Did you see that hideous yellow arch? You see what I have to deal with, what I'm up against? My God, I have to do everything myself."

This was the extent of her conversation with me. She told the band and singers to take a break and then turned her attention to Camden.

"Cam, I can't focus under these conditions. Would you please come assess the aura on this stage?"

"Can you do that?" I asked him. "Are you a licensed Aura Assessor?"

"I'll give it a try."

While Camden checked out any offending auras, I went backstage to check around and was in Sherry's dressing room when she came in, sat down at her mirror, and began to yank at her orange curls.

"Where is that wretched girl who's supposed to fix my hair? First Diamond and now this! The whole world is against me."

"If it's any consolation, I found Diamond," I said.

Sherry dismissed this with a wave of her hand. "Who needs her? Cam is so much better."

I pulled up a chair and sat down. "I need to talk to you about your husband."

She gave me a wry look. "Ex-husband."

"So what's the story?"

She shrugged. "It just didn't work out. I don't expect you to understand."

"I understand. I've been married twice, myself."

This caught her interest. "So what's your story?"

I was not going into the entire saga. "I like being married, I just can't stay married."

"My ex-husband couldn't take my fame. What's your excuse?"

"I have a roving eye."

"Oh, really?" She put her hair up. Now her face looked strangely elongated, like an afghan hound. "I've decided marriage is not for me. I'll just have lovers from now on." She paused and gave me a look. "I suppose you're taken."

I wasn't sure if I was flattered or terrified by that prospect. "I'm in a relationship with a wonderful young woman who brings out the best in me, what little there is."

She swung around to face me squarely. "So what's your problem?"

"Problem?"

"There's always a problem."

"The relationship is solid, but if she can't find a teaching job here, we're going to have to move. Neither of us want to leave our home in Parkland, but we'll think of something." Enough about me. I wanted to hear what Sherry had to say about Mitch Stratton. "Your turn."

She turned back to her mirror and tugged at one of her fake eyelashes. She flicked the eyelash aside and pulled off the other one. For a moment, her expression softened. "I did truly love Mitch, and for a while, everything was wonderful. But then he began to resent my fame. He wanted to call all the shots, and that's just not possible. I'm Sherry White, Incorporated. I have to be in charge, because I'm responsible for the product people buy. If it's not perfect, why bother? Mitch's ideas were haphazard and second rate, absolutely ridiculous. Everything he did was second rate. I could tell right away how to fix things, but he never listened to me. He wanted more control, more power. Then one day he told me he was tired of being in my shadow, so I told him it was time for him to leave."

"Would he send you threatening letters?"

She laughed. "What? Of course not!"

"Did you keep him from having success as an actor?"

"That's nonsense. He didn't want to be an actor."

"What if he did?" I asked. "You had a lot of power. You could've influenced people not to hire him."

She stared at me. "What do you mean, 'had' a lot power?"

"Didn't you shoot down his ideas?"

"His ideas weren't any good!" She returned to my previous statement. "'Had' a lot of power? 'Had'? I'll have you know I can have anyone fired. I could fire you right this minute. Where's my phone? I'm calling that policeman friend of yours and telling him to revoke your backstage pass."

She opened the drawer of her dressing table to search for her phone and let out a long drawn-out shriek. She pointed to a piece of yellow paper curling up from the drawer.

"Oh, my God! Get it away from me!"

I carefully picked up the paper by one corner. Someone had written in large uneven black letters: "Die, you heartless bitch."

Sherry held her arms around herself. Every curl trembled. "How did that get in there? I can't stand this!"

Before I could stop her, she grabbed the letter out of my hands and tore it to pieces.

"Horrible! Horrible!"

"What are you doing?" I said. "Camden might have been able to get something from that."

"I don't want any part of it near me!"

I scooped up some of the pieces. "Sherry, you're going to have to calm down. I can't help you if you're like this."

"Take those pieces out! Take them out now! Bring Cam here. I have to talk to him."

"I'm not doing anything until you shut up and listen."

She drew back with a gasp. Then she closed her mouth and glared.

"During the day, anybody can walk into your dressing room," I said. "Don't you keep it locked while you're on stage?"

"No. Everyone in the company is on stage when I am, the band, the singers, the techies."

"What about the girl who was supposed to fix your hair?"

Sherry's face paled. "I'll kill her, the ungrateful little tramp. I brought her up from nothing, and this is how she repays me."

"I'm not accusing her, I'm just asking about her. She might have seen someone."

Although I imagined that, like Diamond, the hairdresser apparently got tired of wading through the bile and moved on.

"Or planted that awful letter herself," Sherry said.

"Well, if you'd left enough of it, Camden probably could've told you who wrote it."

She tried not to look embarrassed. "Will you take him the pieces and see what he can do?"

"Yes, and next time try to control yourself. We're going to find out who's doing this, I promise, but you have to cooperate. I realize that's a new concept for you, but it works."

She dismissed me with a haughty toss of her head.

I found Camden on stage, chatting with the backup singers. I waited until they left before handing him the pieces. "If you're up to it, somebody sent Sherry another love note, and she's not too happy with it. I know it's not much, but it's all I could salvage from her fury."

Camden turned the pieces over in his hands.

"Anything?" I asked.

"Wild vibes from Sherry."

"She lost it completely. You're going to have to do major damage control. She's really upset." He was silent for such a long time, I added, "Can you handle this or do you want to go home?"

"I'm okay," he said. "It's just that everyone Sherry comes in contact with hates her. It's hard to reconcile that with the person who sings, 'Angel of Love.'"

"It's the alternate universe," I said. "We haven't had that episode yet. You'd be the crude beer-swilling biker."

"You'd be the celibate priest."

"Ellin would be the shy, demure housewife. Too bad we're not on TV. Come calm her majesty."

Sherry apologized profusely to him for destroying the evidence.

"I am so frightened and so furious that anyone would do such a thing."

"I understand," he said. "But if I could touch a whole letter and not just pieces, I might be able to find out who's doing this." He reached for her hand. "Maybe if I held your hand."

She clasped her hands together. "I don't know. I'm so upset. I don't think it will do any good."

"Only for a minute, then."

She reluctantly placed her hand in his, and he stood still for a long moment. Sherry bit her lower lip. She looked even more anxious than before. "What do you see?"

"I'm not sure. There seem to be a lot of Sherry Whites."

"All my costumes changes, of course."

Camden frowned. "Maybe."

"You know I try to be a different person for each song. I live it. I become the music. That must be what you're seeing."

He let go. "Well, it was worth a try."

"What are you going to do now, Randall?" she asked.

"I'm going to talk to your people," I said. "Again."

***

For the second time, I interviewed the crew, the band, the tech people, the roadies and the backup singers. No one had been in Sherry's dressing room. No one had seen anything or anyone suspicious. No one was too particularly upset about the incident.

"What about Sherry's manager?" I asked one of the crew. "Did he or she come on tour?"

"Sherry fired him a couple of months ago," the man said. "Said she'd manage her own affairs from now on."

"And her agent? I'm assuming she has one."

He shook his head. "Fired her, too."

"So she's basically running everything herself."

"Well, we've been on the road with her before, so we know what it takes to get her set up for a concert," he said. "She doesn't put up the stage or set the lights or mess with the sound equipment. As to all the other details, I guess she is taking care of those. The tour's been going as usual."

"Who's looking after the finances?"

"Sherry, I guess. We're still getting paid."

Back in Sherry's dressing room, Camden had calmed her enough that I could ask about her fellow Marigolds, Tracey and Patricia.

"I haven't seen them since we split up," she said. "Tracey died a few years ago."

"Exactly why did you split up? I understand the group was doing really well."

"I wanted a solo career. So did Patricia, but you never hear about her demands, now do you? I'm always the villain. Tracey had a dreadful drug habit, so you can guess where her money went." Her gaze was filled with anxiety. "Did you find out anything from the crew? Maybe one of the security people saw something."

"I have a question about your manager and agent. Is it true you fired them?"

Her glare returned. "What if I did? They weren't doing what I needed them to do."

"Are you planning to replace them, or are you going to run everything by yourself? That's a lot of stress to deal with, isn't it?"

"I might replace them at the end of this tour, if I can find responsible people," she said. "As for the stress, I can handle it."

"Who's looking after Sherry White, Incorporated?" I asked.

"My company shouldn't be your concern. I'm taking care of it."

"I'd like access to your financial records."

For a moment, I thought she'd refuse. "I can't imagine how that would be helpful, but you're welcome to have a look. I'll email you the most recent report. I have nothing to hide." She turned to Camden. "I promise if I find another letter, I won't tear it up. You're coming back for my other rehearsals, aren't you? And the Saturday concert? I can't possibly perform if I don't have you here."

"I'll be here," he said.

"What do you make of all that?" I asked Camden as we got into the Fury. "She keeps finding these letters, but no one has seen or heard anything. You think they're all in this together to drive her crazy?"

"I don't know," he said. "She didn't want me to hold her hand just now."

"Yeah, I noticed. I'd say she was in on the plot, but she seems genuinely frightened."

"She is. I'm just not sure what she's frightened of."

"Then I've got more detecting to do."

He was staring off into space in a way I knew meant trouble.

"You okay?"

"Fine," he said.

"Not planning on getting possessed again, are you?"

He rubbed his forehead. "I've been trying to place that little ghost dancer's music, but nothing's coming to me."

After spending time with Sherry, I was ready for something else. "Let's give it another try."

# CHAPTER THIRTEEN

*"I Don't Feel Like Dancin'"*

In the faint afternoon light, the deserted ballroom looked even more pathetic than I remembered. Camden stood in the middle of the room. I had my phone on video to record the phantom music.

"Let me know when you hear anything," I said.

"Nothing yet."

"Maybe she's on a break, too."

"No, I think she likes popping out and surprising people."

We waited a few moments and then Camden stiffened.

"She's here."

"Any music?"

"The same tune."

I still didn't hear or see anything. Camden hadn't danced with himself two minutes before someone opened the door and called, "Who is in here?"

Camden stopped. "Damn."

Our ghost had flown. An elderly Hispanic man carrying a broom peered in at us suspiciously. "Now, none of that nonsense in here." When he saw Camden, his grim look disappeared and he grinned. "Oh, it's you, Cam. Are you perhaps trying out for the ballet?"

"There's a ghost in here, Marcos," he said. "A young lady, a dancer. I was trying to find out more about her."

Marcos didn't even blink. "Ah, *la pequena bailarina.*"

"You've seen her?"

"*Si, a veces la veo.* Sometimes I see her."

"Any idea why she's here?"

"No," he said. "She does no harm, so I don't worry."

"Do you hear her music?" Camden asked.

"No, no music."

"What can you tell me about this building?" I asked him.

"I don't know as much as I should," he said. "This part we are standing in is part of the old Park Building, built in 1912. The Little Theater was added on later, round about 1962."

"Park, as in Parkland?"

"*Si.* The Park family founded the town sometime in the 1800s. Parkland is named for Charles Park, the first mayor, but you knew that. Everybody knows that."

"What about this ballroom?" I asked. "Can the Historical Society save it?"

"I hope so." He looked around the room. "It must have been beautiful in its day. I do not remember us ever using it, though. It has been closed up for years. Maybe that's why it is haunted. Do you see any more ghosts?"

"Only one," Camden said, "and she sure likes to dance."

"You talk to her, tell her not to cause trouble."

"I will."

He went out. We waited a while longer, but the dancer didn't return.

"You get anything?" Camden asked.

I tried my video. There was nothing except Camden dancing by himself. All we heard was static until the custodian's voice called out, and Camden said, "Damn."

"Can you sing it?" I asked.

He hummed a tune I couldn't quite place.

"I can check through my music," I said, "but you know how many recordings I have. It could take years."

"Marcos said the ballroom was built in 1912," he said. "That should narrow it down a little."

\*\*\*

It was after three when we stopped by the PSN to pick up Elise. Ellin was sitting in her office, Elise tucked in one arm.

Camden gave both of them a kiss. "How was your day?"

"Something very interesting happened," Ellin said in an unusually calm voice. "During today's taping, one of the globes decided to move."

The globes were a set of crystal paperweights that decorated the table on the set. They were colorful and shiny, the very thing to attract a baby.

"I noticed the globe moved when Elise waved her hands and stopped when she stopped." Ellin looked down at Elise and then back at Camden as if daring him to lie. "She's telekinetic, too, isn't she?"

"I told you she would be."

There was a long pause. Then Camden said, "You're okay with this, aren't you?"

"I am more than okay," she said, beaming. "I can't wait for everyone to see her. Can you imagine the ratings? Why, we'd have sponsors lined up for a chance to advertise on the PSN."

Uh, oh. If she couldn't get Camden to perform on the network, the next best thing—maybe even a better thing—would be Elise, the Amazing Telekinetic Baby. I waited to see how Camden would handle things. But he had to have known this would be her reaction.

"Well," he said slowly. "I'm not sure that's a good idea. As for sponsors, I did what you asked and charmed them all."

"Even that crazy little woman at the pet store?"

"Yes, and all the crazy people at Lunch in a Can. They aren't leaving."

"We need more sponsors than we have, anyway," she said. "Having Elise on one of my shows is the answer."

The last thing Camden wanted was to have Elise or any of his future children exploited on TV. "How about this?" he asked. "Why don't you stay home with Elise for a while and enjoy her while she's a baby? We'll see how her talent progresses and then make a decision."

"And what exactly would we do for money if I stay at home?"

"We'll manage."

She sighed. "I knew this was going to be a problem. Maybe you can manage on peanut butter and tuna and second hand sneakers, but I can't, and I don't want Elise to settle for second best. I don't want all her clothes to come from Special Delivery Consignments or yard sales. Besides, this was not part of our deal. I keep my job. You keep Elise."

"Elise doesn't care where her clothes come from," Camden said. "I don't care. Who are you trying to impress? Nobody looks at the labels in baby clothes, for goodness sake."

"Cam, I am not going to argue with you about Elise's clothes. It's more than that, and you know it." Elise made a whimpering noise, and Ellin rearranged the blanket around her. "You want new clothes, don't you?" she asked the baby. "Not some other baby's clothes."

Camden decided to dive off the high board. "I don't want her on TV."

She cut her eyes around so fast I instinctively ducked to avoid the death ray. "What?"

"I don't want Elise to be on TV. Not now. Not ever."

"Camden." His name came out as a growl from between her teeth.

"If people see her moving things, they'll either accuse you of faking it for ratings, or they'll swarm the studio wanting pictures, and then the media will get hold of the story and we'll never have a moment's peace. I'd be terrified that someone would kidnap her."

Ellin kept her arms around Elise, whose little face wore an expression of extreme concern. She spoke sarcastically. "Did all this come to you in a vision?"

"No, I figured it out for myself."

"Well, it's all terribly tragic, but it's not going to happen. We'll finally have enough money, and I'll have a very nice new home and that's where Elise will be. You can join us if you feel like it."

Elise burst into tears, and from the look on Camden's face, I knew he felt the same. Ellin had always been a social climber, but I'd never realized how far she'd go to advance her career.

"You can't mean that," Camden said.

Ellin can change gears faster than a champion NASCAR race driver. She stood, rocked the baby gently, and leaned over her to kiss him.

"Oh, God, that was a rotten thing to say. I'm sorry. We've got to find some way around this."

He returned her kiss. "If you'll just calm down. All three kids are going to have some kind of talent."

She paused. "Are you absolutely sure we're going to have two more children?"

"You know I am."

"How can you know? You always tell me your future is indistinct."

"But I can see *your* future."

She was much more interested in the future of her career. "Please tell me the PSN is going to succeed."

I had to butt in. "You will always be their queen," I said. "You don't need Elise for that."

She gave me her best exasperated sigh. "Randall, I don't really think this is your business."

"Are you kidding? Ever since I moved here, everything in this house has been my business."

"But aren't you and Kary planning to move?" she asked.

"Not if I can help it. Would you please save everyone a lot of trouble and reconsider putting Elise on TV?"

Her eyes narrowed. "That's something Camden and I will take care of. Aren't you supposed to be investigating these threatening letters someone's sending to Sherry White?"

"Yes," I said. "I'm on the case."

"Then you stick to that and let me take care of matters at the PSN. And speaking of Sherry White, just how dangerous is this letter-writer?"

"That's what I'm trying to find out."

"Then get to it."

I gave her a salute. "Yes, ma'am. Anything to report on Diamond?"

"I don't think this is significant," she said. "On her break, all Diamond did was talk on her phone."

"Any idea who she called?"

"I assumed it was her boyfriend. She laughed and giggled and said she'd found another job. She said 'sweetie' and 'honey' and 'see you soon.'"

"Okay, good job."

This stopped her for a moment. Then she said, "Thank you. Do you want me to continue?"

"Yes, if it's not too much trouble."

I had the strangest feeling she wanted to say, "I'd love to!" but she what she really said was, "All right."

# CHAPTER FOURTEEN

### *"Stolen Dance"*

At home, Camden and Ellin took the baby and went upstairs to continue the peace talks. I went to my office to search through my vast collection of ragtime and traditional jazz tapes and CDs. I had narrowed my search to a few hundred choices when Kary stopped by my door.

"Good news," she said. "The Mooresville Central Office finally called. They said some major staffing issues have come up so it may be several days, maybe even a week, before they need my answer. This should give me extra time to look for something closer. What a relief!"

Relief didn't half cover my feelings on this matter.

"But I don't want to get too hopeful that the perfect job will turn up. I want a snack and some mindless TV." She glanced in my office door at the piles of tapes and CDs. "Are you rearranging your music?"

"A young dancer is haunting the ballroom behind the Little Theater. Camden can hear her music, and he says it's a ragtime tune. Know anything about the Park Building?"

"No, but I'll be happy to find out."

The little fragment of song Camden remembered repeated itself in my head, just on the edge of memory. As much as I love ragtime and traditional jazz, I'll admit a lot of it sounds the same. I knew it wasn't a hard driving song like the New Black Eagle Jazz Band plays. Something more along the lines of Scott Joplin, but more haunting. That was the word. There was a "Haunting Rag," and a "Sleepy Hollow Rag," and a tune called "Graceful Ghost," but I knew those tunes, and the little dancer's song that Camden hummed for me wasn't any of these.

I needed a break. Kary fixed popcorn and we settled together on the sofa and turned on the TV. Kary took the remote and began channel surfing. She paused on one of the movie channels. "Oh, look. Sherry White in *Days of Splendor.*"

Sherry White glowered from the television, looking distinctly out of place in some sort of French Revolution costume and singing away.

"Is she supposed to be Marie Antoinette?"

Kary turned down the sound to spare me from hearing the song. "She's a poor farm girl in disguise. She's infiltrating the court to save her lover. We can change channels if you'd rather not watch it."

"No, it looks fascinating."

I'm not sure what Kary would've replied because our attention was caught by the action on screen. Even with the sound down, Sherry White's shrieking came through.

"What the hell's going on?" I asked.

"Oh, this is the most exciting part." She took the remote and turned up the volume. "She's gone down to the dungeons to rescue Pierre, and she has to convince the guards she's the queen."

"By screaming at them?"

"By showing the royal temper."

"I'll say." I'd seen that face and heard that tone.

"How dare you accost me? How dare you impede my progress? Do you not know who I am? I have every right to walk where I choose! I wish to interrogate this prisoner, and I do not need your help. Begone!"

One of the guards, like an idiot, tried to reply. "But, your majesty—"

"Silence! I will have no more of this impudence! If you value your positions in this court and your lives, you will leave at once!"

Man, sounded just like backstage. The guards retreated. Sherry and Pierre clung to the bars of his prison and began to sing something about I'll never leave you, you are my life, no prison can hold our love, blah, blah, blah.

"Isn't all this singing going to tip off the guards?" I asked.

"You'd think so, wouldn't you? It happens in all her movies, and the bad guys never catch on." She turned the sound down.

I had an idea. "How many of Sherry's movies do you have?"

"All of them."

"Let me see."

Kary looked through the collection of DVDs stacked beside the TV, found what she wanted, and handed the plastic cases to me. "What are you looking for?"

According to the information on the back of the cases, Sherry's movies were produced by Crystal Clear Productions. "Something Sherry told me when we were discussing Mitch," I said. "She told me his ideas were haphazard and second rate and she was the only one who could fix them. Mitch's failed company was called Crystal Films. I wonder if Sherry took over Crystal

Films and rebranded it."

It didn't take long for Kary to find that Crystal Clear Productions started right after Crystal Films folded. Crystal Clear Productions specialized in concert films, not only of Sherry, but of some of the more current and popular musical acts and small independent movies, the kind of movies Sherry said Mitch Stratton suggested she try. I wondered if he was aware of this move and how it made him feel. Not good would be my guess.

"Looks like once Mitch got the boot, Sherry took over the company, changed its name, and started doing the very things Mitch wanted to do," I said.

"I would imagine he's not very happy about that," Kary said.

"I would imagine you're right. I also imagine she did the same thing to Images."

Kary's fingers flew across the laptop's keyboard. "Let's see if we can find out."

It didn't take her long to find a likely match. "What about this?" she said, indicating a website called Visions. "This one produces documentaries like the ones you described."

Not only did Visions produce documentaries like the ones I described, it produced documentaries *exactly* like the ones I described: Bedouin tribesmen in the Sahara, a riverboat exploring the Amazon, and rice farmers in China. The subject matter was the same, but the camera work was superior to Mitch's. It was almost as if Sherry was saying, "In your face, buster," and bursting into a chorus of "Anything You Can Do, I Can Do Better."

"Okay. This is serious," I said and explained how Visions was a copy of Images.

"Wow, that's low," Kary said. "So if Mitch is aware of this takeover, he could very well be the letter writer."

"And there was another letter today. She was already in volcano mode when she found it. I'm surprised you didn't feel the aftershocks. This one said, 'Die, you heartless bitch.'"

Kary grimaced. "I'd be upset, too."

"Trouble is she tore the letter to shreds before Camden had a chance to hold it, so her exploding vibes destroyed any clue we might have found."

Kary frowned in thought. "Are you sure it said, 'Die, you heartless bitch'? I read something similar in the *Galaxy*."

"You read the tabloids? I'm shocked."

"Sometimes you just have to."

"Well, the *Galaxy* is on the ball," I said. "Do you happen to have any issues here?"

"I'm embarrassed to say I do."

She went into the kitchen and rooted through the recyclables until she found the paper she wanted. She handed me the tabloid folded back to the story I wanted to read.

It was titled "Star Continues Bravely Despite Life-Threatening Letters."

"'Glamorous singer Sherry White was recently terrorized by yet another poison-pen note. This letter contained a message that read, "You should die, you heartless bitch." Despite these vile threats to her life and well-being, Miss White bravely plans to continue her concert tour, and expresses her love and affection for her fans who continue to stand by her during this difficult time. Police and private investigators remain stumped as to the identity of the mysterious letter-writer.'"

Even more interesting was the by-line for the story: Tony Kenner.

"Kary, when did you start reading about Sherry in the *Galaxy*?

Before 'Angel of Love' came out? Before her tour?"

"Yes, a month or two maybe. I thought the letters were from a crazy fan. You never know what people are going to do these days."

"No, you surely don't. But in this case, I think the only crazy person is Sherry White, crazy enough to fuel her own publicity machine with lots of ink from a poison pen."

"She's writing her own hate mail?"

"And sending it to Tony Kenner. That's why he was hanging around the auditorium the other day. He said he had an interview with Sherry. I think he was there to pick up the next installment of 'Star Continues Bravely.'"

"Is she really that desperate?"

"You should have seen her rip that letter to shreds. Even Camden wasn't able to put together any of the words. 'Wild vibes from Sherry,' he'd said. Sure. Because it was another overly-dramatic performance to distract from her real purpose."

On screen, Sherry had freed Pierre and the two of them were dashing through the royal gardens to the waiting carriage that was their getaway car. Both Sherry and the actor playing Pierre looked believably concerned, dare I even say desperate?

"I've thought of something else." I reached for my phone. "When Jordan hired me for security, he was the one who told me Sherry had received threatening letters. Wonder how his case is coming along?" I reached for my phone.

Jordan sounded unimpressed by Sherry's predicament. "What's wrong with her majesty now?"

"Sherry found another note in her dressing room today, but she tore it up before Camden could get a good read on it."

"Sounds like her. You notice any suspicious characters wandering around backstage? Any real tangible threats?"

"I think she's feeding info to Tony Kenner for publicity."

"Well, fortunately for her, she never filed a formal report," he said. "Filing a false claim isn't looked on very kindly here at the Parkland Police Department."

"So you didn't take her case?"

"What case? Other than that letter we got from Valerie Banner, there's no evidence her life's in danger. If she truly feels threatened, she should call us."

He ended the call. I turned to Kary. "Sherry never filed a police report."

"So this is a publicity stunt."

"Yep. I will confront my client tomorrow."

She put her arms around me. "Then you will need some serious loving to fortify you for the battle ahead."

# CHAPTER FIFTEEN

*"Ladies of the Dance"*

Wednesday morning, I found a note on my desk from Kary.

"Off to the library to research the Park Building. Love, Velma."

When Kary first started helping on cases, she told me in no uncertain terms she was not going to be the Velma of our Scooby Gang, but now she didn't mind doing research if she also got to disguise herself and run around at night.

Before I did anything else, I checked the Parkland City Schools webpage. The school system was looking for a P.E. teacher, a math teacher for the high school, three Special Education teachers, a speech pathologist, computer teachers, and vocational skills teachers. I called the Parkland Schools Central Office, and a pleasant sounding woman assured me they had Miss Ingram's name on file and would notify her the minute a teaching or guidance counselor position became available.

"If she can wait, it's not unusual for positions to open right at the beginning of the school year. We'll make every effort to find a place for her, but Parkland is a very popular school system, I'm pleased to say."

I did the same thing for the school systems in Celosia and other towns close by. I even checked out the private schools. Nothing. I didn't have much luck with Patricia Lansdale, either. I called again and got the same message on her machine. I left another message, asking her to call me.

Sherry had sent me the latest financial report from Sherry White, Incorporated. It took a while to wade through all the facts and figures, but I could see that sales of Sherry's CDs and concert tickets had dipped considerably in the past year, with a slight increase starting three months ago, about the time she received her first threatening letter.

Next I went to Sherry's web page and looked around. I had several choices: Sherry's life story, tour dates and ticket info, products with Sherry's name or picture on them, ranging from coffee mugs to sparkly tee shirts, a movie page, Sherry's new projects, and a chat room for fans. I read Sherry's life story, from the struggling but loving family who adopted her in Middleton, Pennsylvania, to the heights of the recording world. I checked out the new projects page and read that Sherry's latest song, "Love, Youth, and Beauty," would be out next month. Then I decided to see what the fans were talking about on Facebook and Twitter.

Besides the usual gushing, there were comments about Sherry's latest crisis and many theories. One fan, who called herself sherrysbiggestfan, thought the letters might be from a rival diva. Another, lovesherryforever, said it was a plot by the recording company to make Sherry record the songs the company wanted. Still another, who went by the initials SBFF—Sherry's Best Friend Forever, I guessed—thought Sherry had angered a group of radicals who wanted only rap and rock music on the radio. I scrolled further down, finding more of the same. There was no mention of Crystal Clear Productions or Visions, Sherry's latest acquisition.

I fixed myself some toast and coffee and headed out to the porch. Camden sat in the swing, Elise in his lap, his usual breakfast of brown sugar Pop-Tarts and Coke on the wicker table. I sat down in one of the rocking chairs. Cardinals and sparrows argued over the seeds in the bird feeder. Cindy sat on the porch railing, watching them, her tail twitching. Oreo observed from between the railings. I'm sure he thought he was invisible.

Elise opened and closed her hands, but I didn't see anything hop, roll, or sail around the porch.

"She's still figuring it out," Camden said.

"Tell her to let it rest for a couple of years," I said. "That'll give you time to work on a convincing argument as to why she shouldn't have her own show on the PSN—although *Telekinesis With Elise* would be a great title."

"Not going to happen." He reached over to the table for his Coke and took a drink. "Any progress this morning?"

I grimaced. "Very meager results."

"'Meager.' You don't hear that every day. Spell it."

"What is this, an additional challenge? M-e-a-g-e-r. Do you even know if I'm right or not? And do I get extra points for this?"

"I never said I could spell."

The sparrows now had position on the feeder and were using this advantage to stuff themselves. "Let's see," I said. "There are no teaching jobs available in the entire state, Patricia Lansdale is still unavailable, and Sherry has done her best to ruin Mitch's career." I filled him in on what Kary and I had discovered.

"So that makes him an excellent candidate for Revengeful Correspondent," Camden said.

The cardinals won the Battle of the Feeder and sat puffed up and proud of themselves. "Yes, although I still have my suspicions about Tony Kenner. I thought I'd head over to the *Galaxy* today."

"Let me change Elise's diaper and we'll come with you."

"You're taking a telekinetic baby into the offices of the *Galaxy News Weekly*? We're looking at the story of the year. Ellin will be so jealous."

"I doubt anyone at the *Galaxy* will notice if Elise shows off."

Camden took Elise into the house about the time Lily came through the break in the hedge, followed by Denny. I don't know which of them looked more dazzling. Lily had on a pink suit and matching heels, pink lipstick, and eye shadow, her hair swept up into some fancy bun. She looked like the tiny executive president of a major corporation. Denny was wearing a dark shiny cocktail dress with a flared skirt. A small hat with a veil perched on his head. They looked like they were on their way to tea at the Plaza.

"Ladies, I am impressed," I said. "Lily, you look fantastic."

She blushed. "Thank you."

Denny beamed with pride and brushed the shoulder of Lily's suit as if to remove any trace of lint. "I'm going to take her to the Pyramid and show her off."

"You've done a great job," I said. "Not that you weren't pretty before, Lily, but you really look sensational in that suit."

"She has all these darling outfits in her closet that she never wears," Denny said. "We're going to try them all. And she'd never worn a scrap of makeup!"

"It doesn't really last on long voyages," Lily said.

Denny rolled his eyes. "What did I tell you about that? Those aliens don't have a chance against me. Why, I'm more alien than anyone in the galaxy. Now where's Cam?" he asked. "We want him to see us in all our finery."

"He's changing Elise."

"Lily, dearest, have a seat. We'll wait out here and surprise him."

Lily sat down in the other rocking chair while Denny spread his skirt and took over the porch swing.

When Camden came back he stopped. "Lily, is that you? Wow, I didn't recognize you!"

She got up and turned around so he could get the full view. "Do you like it? I feel so different."

"You look wonderful," he said. "But do you like it?"

She gave Denny a shy glance. "I didn't at first, but now I do. I can always go back to my other clothes if I want."

"No, we're going to throw all those away," Denny said with a large gesture.

"Denny, you promised."

"Just teasing, dearest."

"I really like my green jumper."

"We shall make a shrine."

She gave his hand a little slap. "You silly thing."

Camden turned wide eyes to me at this exchange. "Well, I'm glad you two are having fun with fashion," I said.

Denny stood, rearranged his skirt, and took Lily's hand. "Now we're off to the Pyramid. See you later, boys."

He escorted Lily out to his yellow LeBaron, opened the door, and tucked her in. As they drove off, Camden shook his head.

"I never thought I'd see Lily without a hat."

"More has changed besides her clothes."

"He's exactly right for her. I don't know why I didn't see it before."

"No one could've seen it," I said. I took one last drink of coffee. "While they make their Pyramid debut, let's go see what's happening at the *Galaxy*."

# CHAPTER SIXTEEN

## *"Could I Have This Dance?"*

If the offices of the *Galaxy* weren't the epicenter of hell, they could be definitely be considered one of the lower circles. In the reception area, some of the better headlines from previous issues had been framed and put on display, including "President's Secret Love Child Caught in Neo Nazi Sting" and "Terrorists Attack Mastermind From Atlantis." We asked to see Jake Banner, and the receptionist, a buxom young woman liberally sprinkled with tattoos, told us to have a seat. All the folding chairs were occupied, most of them by people in outlandish costumes. Several grim looking farmers clutching misshapen vegetables stood along one wall. Beyond the reception area was a buzz of conversations and a clatter of computer keys.

"Yo! Randall!"

Jake Banner came strolling through all the chaos, grinning. "How you doing? And this must be Camden." He held out his hand. "Pleasure to meet you, pal. Big fan."

"Thanks," Camden said.

Jake didn't shake hands for long. "No offense, but I heard

about that little trick of yours. I got too many secrets that need to stay secret." Elise gazed up at him from her baby front pack, and he gave her a big smile. "Who's this cute little accessory you're wearing?"

"This is Elise."

"Come on back! You don't have to hang out with the regulars."

He led us through a maze of desks. Although each desk had a computer, no one seemed to be working. Instead, the reporters were calling out ideas across the room.

"Hey! Have we done an end-of-the-world story this month?"

"What about that new starlet's drug habit? Didn't she sell her blood? Or was that her baby?"

"It can be both," Jake called back, grinning. "Or even her baby's blood—pardon me, Elise."

"Good one, Jake!"

"How was the Bermuda Triangle?" I asked.

He shrugged. "Oh, the usual. I prefer Stonehenge, myself."

We reached a desk that was obviously Jake's, judging from the colorful array of plastic aliens and model space ships. "Kenner's not here," he said, "but we can go through his desk."

An inspection of Kenner's desk turned up a pencil, a few paper clips, and a couple of dead flies.

"Are you sure he still works here?" I asked.

"Haven't heard otherwise."

Out of the corner of my eye, I saw one of Jake's more brightly colored toy spaceships rising unevenly from his desk. Camden gently covered Elise's hand with his own, and the spaceship landed.

I took a couple of steps around Kenner's desk to block Jake's view. "Where does Kenner hang out when he isn't here?"

"Any bar in town, adult film and bookstores, A.J.'s pool hall. The usual clichés for a slimeball. You'd hardly expect to find him at Mother Mary's Cupcake Parlor."

"Hey, Jake!" someone called from the depths of the room. "There's some guy here to see you. Says it's about a haunted house."

Jake's eyes lit up. "That's my wall feeler! See you later, fellas."

He hurried off. "A wall feeler?" I said to Camden.

"That would be someone who feels walls."

"I have no use for that, but I need a female voice for my cunning plan. I always sound like Mickey Mouse when I try it. Do you think Kary could sound like Sherry?"

"I know someone even better," he said.

I snapped my fingers. "Denny, of course. He said he impersonated Sherry in his act."

"I'm sure he'll be glad to help."

\*\*\*

We decided Elise didn't need to go into bars or A.J.'s pool hall, so she stayed in the car with Camden while I went into the various establishments to inquire about Kenner. In the pool hall, A.J. told me the last time Kenner had stopped by, he'd been in high spirits and bragged about a "big score" coming up, but wouldn't share many details.

"Still working for the *Galaxy*?" I asked.

"Yeah, but he acted like that wouldn't be for long. When I asked him if his big score included a promotion to the *Herald*, he scoffed and said, 'This'll be way better than anything in the *Herald*. I'm talking major exposure, all the national news outlets.' Then he said, 'But I gotta keep everything on the down low. Nobody's stealing my scoop. It's my ticket out of the 'bloids.'"

When I related this to Camden, he said, "But if Sherry's problem isn't making the national news now, why would Kenner think his big score would?"

"That's a good question," I said, "unless this big score is something worse than letters."

\*\*\*

We went back home to get some lunch and a bottle or two for Elise. She was halfway through her first bottle when Kary called to say she and Mandy, the reference librarian, had found several books that might have the information I needed on the Park Building ballroom. So after Elise was full, Camden and I stopped by the Parkland Public Library and went downstairs to the reference department. By then, Elise was asleep in her front pack, so I didn't have to worry about books and magazines taking flight.

Mandy was an earnest little woman with a cloud of pale hair who enjoyed helping out on my cases as much as Kary. If Mandy didn't know the answer—and she usually did—she knew where to find it. After admiring the baby, she plopped three large black books and another book bound in red leather on the desk. "The entire history of Parkland."

She handed me one black book and gave Kary another. Camden took the red book, and we started our search. Mandy was quicker, of course, using time-honored librarian techniques, like checking the table of contents and index. She soon found several old photos of the building. One was of the ground-breaking ceremony in 1912; one showed the building half-finished; one showed the whole street with the completed Park Building outlined. Kary found an article about the construction companies involved, how the funds were raised from various textile and agricultural corporations, and what the building would be used for. Only one mention was made of the ballroom, which she read aloud.

"A spacious ballroom has been added, and will no doubt be the site of many grand balls to commemorate our fair city's accomplishments and events."

In the red leather book, which covered the city's history from 1940 to 1970, Camden found photos and articles about the Park Building being remodeled for the theater. Nothing was said about the ballroom. No fires, earthquakes, disasters, or scandals, nothing that would cause a ghost to return for revenge or closure.

Mandy saw my puzzled expression. "I'll keep looking, David. There are a lot of old newspaper clippings on microfiche. No one ever uses them, so they're kind of in a mess. We've been meaning to re-organize them. This will give me a good excuse."

"Thanks," I said.

"I'm curious about your ghost. What's it like?"

"You'll have to ask Camden."

"It's a young woman in a ball gown," he said. "So far, all she's done is dance. There wasn't a ballet school, was there, or some dancer who was murdered or committed suicide?"

"I'll do my best to find out," Mandy said.

"Maybe she came to a costume ball. We were thinking turn of the century, but she could be a modern woman in a costume. Maybe she was in a play and died tragically."

I closed my reference book. "It may not be anything, at all. She doesn't seem to be a threat."

"Is she warning you about something?" Mandy asked.

"No, she's just dancing," I said. "It's going to bug me till I figure out her music. It's a ragtime tune, I know that."

"1912 is when they began building everything," Kary said. "I'm sure there's a book that lists the popular music of each year."

"We have quite a few," Mandy said.

"Plus there's always Google."

She grinned. "Yes, a good librarian uses every tool at her disposal. Come on, Kary. The game's afoot—and online."

\*\*\*

Elise was still fast asleep when Camden settled her into her car seat. "I'm sure Valerie would be happy to do Sherry's voice for you," he said.

This time I employed the Dark Look. "Don't even think about it." I checked my watch. "Give Denny a call and see if he's available."

Denny reported that he and Lily had been a huge success at the Pyramid and that they were on their way to the theater for his dance rehearsal. He'd be glad to see us there.

"I'm not sure I need another round of Bizarro World Bali Ha'i," I said.

"Let's give the little ghost dancer another try," Camden said.

So I revved up the Fury and we headed for the theater and the ballroom.

\*\*\*

This time, I saw her.

The white blur in the center of the room gradually took form, and there, pirouetting gracefully in the center of the darkness, was a dainty white female figure. Her filmy white dress rose and fell in languid waves about her slim transparent body. Her long white hair moved as if afloat in a sea current. I watched as she glided about the room, unable to follow the quick steps of her blurred feet. When she saw me, she stopped and approached, but whether or not she recognized me from before, I couldn't tell.

How to explain the lovely apparition dancing gracefully around Camden to approach me? "Camden, I see her. What now?"

Her features were blurred like an out-of-focus film, but there seemed to be an expression of impish delight on the young woman's face as she curtsied, her filmy gown billowing.

I looked to Camden for instructions. "Bow," he said.

I bowed. The young woman's left hand settled lightly as a snowflake on my shoulder. Her right hand lay in mine like a wisp of cloud. That's when I heard the music, a plaintive, slightly sinister minor tune.

"I hear the music."

"Can you dance?" Camden asked.

"Sort of."

"Try a few rounds. Then I'll cut in."

The last time I'd danced was at my first wedding. The ghost girl didn't seem to mind my awkwardness. Her face was alight, clear eyes shining with the sheer joy of moving to the music. She appeared to be about sixteen. Her gown was definitely early 1900s. It was oddly exhilarating to guide this lighter-than-air lady around the room.

"Nice to meet you," I said. "My name's David. Come here often?"

She didn't answer. She closed her eyes, her mouth in a half-smile.

When Camden cut in, the music transposed to a more cheerful key, and around they went, the young woman executing elaborate moves within the circle of his arms. Then she left him and circled lazily back to me, eyes still closed as if she were dreaming of dancing. Then she opened her eyes and faced me, arms out, beckoning.

"Nope," I said. "No more dancing. Tell me what you want. I'm pretty good at finding things. What is it? Old boyfriend? Deed to the mansion? Your special diamond ring? You have to leave before they tear down this ballroom, or you'll have nowhere to go."

She danced up to me and paused, her features shifting in and out of focus. She curtsied, all filmy lace, a flower opening.

"Tell me."

Her eyes held my gaze. Her mouth quirked in a smile. She danced away and left me for Camden. She curtsied and waited, her gown and hair drifting about her. Camden took her around the ballroom a couple of times.

"Anything?" I asked as they passed by.

"All she wants to do—"

"—is dance. Yes, we've established that."

The dancer smiled as if accepting this as a compliment, twirled once, and disappeared.

\*\*\*

Fortunately, Denny's dance rehearsal was almost over, so we only had to watch a short psychedelic version of "Happy Talk." The chorus carried huge neon flowers and pineapples and they swirled about while Denny as Bloody Harry and Whitley's niece as Liat made hand gestures to the lyrics. Afterwards, Denny and Lily met us in the parking lot. I explained what I wanted him to do, and he was delighted to be of service.

I handed him a piece of paper. "Here's what I'd like you to say."

Denny read what I'd written, his eyes getting wide. "Dear me! You are a descriptive person, David! But I'm up to the challenge."

"Great. Here we go." I punched in Kenner's number. When the answering machine picked up, I handed my phone to Denny.

"Tony, this is Sherry," he said in a passable imitation of her lofty tone. "There's another letter, and it says, 'I'd like to rip out your larynx with a claw hammer.' Truly dreadful, but it's bound to sell papers. I'll talk to you later." He handed the phone to me. "Do you really think Sherry and this scumbag reporter are in cahoots?"

"That's what we'll find out," I said. "Nice job."

"Thank you. So she tells him what to write, and what, pays him to do it?"

"I can't see Tony Kenner doing anything for free. He gets paid, and she gets publicity."

"What if he gets this message and then checks with Sherry for more details?"

"I don't think he will," I said. "He's got a deadline. All he needs is some kind of quote from her, and if she doesn't call, I'll bet he can make up his own."

Lily looked troubled. "But what if you're wrong and there really is a crazed letter writer?"

"If there really is, I don't know how he or she is getting into her dressing room. No one in the cast or crew wants to be anywhere near Sherry, especially when she's on a tear. You should see her flip out when she finds a letter. It's quite a show. All this horror has to be an act."

"Well, she's known for her dramatic roles," Denny said.

"Overly dramatic, I'd say. Last night, Kary and I watched one of her movies. Sherry doesn't have a lot of range, but she can pitch an Oscar-worthy fit." I turned to Camden. "No wonder she tore the letters up. If you had enough to go on, you might discover her secret. Whenever you held her hand or a letter or a piece of one, what do you see?"

"Different versions of Sherry."

"Exactly. I thought she was still upset about the latest letter, but she was afraid you'd see the truth. You were seeing her in all her roles, including distraught diva."

"Dear me," Denny said. "It seems a complicated way to get her name in the papers."

"She must be pretty desperate for a comeback," Camden said.

Denny tugged at one eye. "Excuse me, I think I'm losing a lash. Whoops, there it is. Got it. And she has a new song coming out soon. All the boys were talking about it. 'Young Love's Beauty,' or something like that."

"'Love, Youth, and Beauty,'" I said. "I saw it on her website."

"That's it. Exciting news. But it'll have to do really well to beat all the new little divas out there. The boys also tell me Sherry's tour isn't going as well as she'd like. Why is she staying a whole week in Parkland?"

"She says she needs to meditate. She took a seminar at one of the spas in town."

"The boys say rumor has it she had a breakdown."

"I wouldn't be surprised."

Denny fluffed his hair. "Well, as much as I admire Sherry, I'm not sure she can run with the pack any more. She'd have to work hard to top that new singer's 'Love Me Beyond Forever.' What is her name? Something quite peculiar but still lovely. She took six or seven awards this year. It's been a while since Sherry won an award."

With her tour and a new song, Sherry needed loads of publicity and apparently didn't care if the publicity was good or bad. "We'll wait and see if Kenner takes the bait," I said. Then I'd know for sure how far Sherry White would go.

# CHAPTER SEVENTEEN

*"Shadow Dancing"*

Thursday morning I called Jason Frost to set up a time for Katarina to have her picture taken. He said we could come right away if that suited Ms Klomsky, which it did.

When we arrived, he took one look at Kary in all her faded hippie glory and said, "I have just the backdrop for you, Ms Klomsky."

"Katarina, please," she said, heavy on the accent.

"If you'll give me one moment. My apologies, but I need to sign just a few more pictures."

She waved a languid hand. "Of course."

"Please come have a seat."

He led us to his studio. Kary took a slow walk around, admiring the framed photos on the wall. I ambled over to have a look at his latest photos spread out on his desk, black and white pictures of clouds and trees. Frost took a very small paintbrush and appeared to be writing his name on the prints.

"You autograph each picture?" I asked.

"I have a little symbol I like to put down in the corner of my photographs," he said. "That way people know they're getting a genuine Jason Frost."

The symbol was a stylized "J" and "F" drawn to look like one letter. I took a closer look at the photo of Sherry. "When did you say you'd photographed Sherry White?"

"At least ten years ago."

In the background of the picture, I saw people gathered about holding beer bottles and champagne glasses. "Were you at a party?"

"Yes, I used to have parties in my loft in New York. A lot of my portraits were taken as candid shots. I don't like stiff formal poses."

"Were the other Marigolds invited?"

"I'm sure they were. Everyone was invited whether they were famous or not. I think that's where Sherry met Mitch Stratton."

"Was he into film making then?" I asked.

"Yes, he was always shooting little movies of our parties. Probably gave Sherry the idea to pursue a film career."

"Do you have any copies of these little movies?"

"No. I imagine Sherry does."

I imagined Sherry didn't, not if she and Stratton were through.

Frost put another stack of photos on his desk. He picked one from the top of the stack. "Now this is from my series called 'Childhood Wonders.' I'm particularly proud of this one. It won first prize at the Photography Fair last year."

It was a picture of a child, a color photograph. A beautiful little girl sat under a tree, her dark hair backlit by the sun so she appeared to be wearing a halo. Golden leaves spiraled down around her, and in her lap, a tiny black kitten gazed up.

For a moment, I couldn't breathe. Lindsey had a little black kitten named Shadow. After she died, it ran away.

*It's all right, Daddy. I found Shadow.*

Lindsey's voice, as clear as the sunlight in the photo.

Frost took my silence for admiration. "I know," he said. "Caught the light just right, just as that kitten looked up. It's a stunning picture, even if I say so myself. I actually photographed that same little girl in scenes for all four seasons." He started going through the stack. "Building a snowman, making a daisy chain, and for summer, I found a lovely rose garden with a fountain for her to play in. She's my brother's youngest. Quite the charmer. Let me show you."

He pulled out the summer picture. There was indeed a lovely rose garden and a fountain, but superimposed over the photograph of his brother's youngest was another little girl with long brown curls and a white lace dress. Lindsey seemed to step out of the picture. She wavered before me, not as clear as in dreams, but definitely there, Shadow tucked in one arm.

*I know you can help the little dancer, Daddy. I told her you would.*

Frost had turned his attention to Kary. Neither of them gave any indication of seeing or hearing Lindsey. He had taken an ornate vase filled with artificial flowers and trailing ivy and set it on a small marble topped table. Kary arranged herself on a low sofa and settled her fringed shawl around her.

"Let that fall off one shoulder," Frost said from behind his camera. "Yes, that's lovely. And turn your head so you're looking at the flowers. Perfect."

Once again, I heard Lindsey's voice. *She wants you to find her song, Daddy. She's forgotten.*

I'm working on it, I thought back to her. Is that all she wants? Will that help her move on?

*You need to find it. It's important. Her family is waiting for her.*

You know I'll do everything I can.

"Yes, very nice," Frost said to Kary. "Now one facing me. Lovely. Let's try the same pose without your glasses. Good. One more to the side. Yes. And one more looking away. Gaze off in the distance as if you're remembering a fond memory."

Lindsey playing with Shadow in our backyard, the backyard of our perfect home. Autumn leaves falling from the trees. Shadow leaping and pouncing in a frenzy to catch them. Lindsey clapping her hands in delight. Barbara and I watching from the back porch, laughing at the kitten's antics, our rocking chairs close together.

Lindsey smiled again and faded.

"Come look at these, David," Kary said in her Katarina voice. "I believe Jason has captured my essence."

I took a few steadying breaths and walked over to her.

"I can't possibly choose a favorite," she said. "I love them all."

Jason turned the camera so I could see the images. Kary looked like a woman from another time, a Bohemian princess or an ethereal gypsy. "Stunning," I said.

"They turned out beautifully," Frost said. "Katarina is very photogenic."

"Thank you," she said. She gave me such a curious look, I wondered if my emotions were showing. "Let us decide on a price. David, you may wait in the car. I won't be long."

I was grateful for a few minutes alone. When she came out of the house, she paused to give Frost another graceful pageant-like wave, and then slid into the passenger seat of the Fury.

"Are you okay?"

"I am now," I said. "I saw Lindsey."

"Saw her? Well, that's unusual, isn't it?"

"I was glad to see her, I just—some memories caught me by surprise."

She nodded, her warm brown eyes full of sympathy. I started the car and drove back toward home. She didn't say anything else. She didn't have to.

\*\*\*

At home, Kary changed out of her Katarina disguise and offered to look for more songs. I wanted a word with Diamond. Camden and Elise decided to join me on a trip to the PSN studio. Once there, Elise needed a diaper changed, so while Camden took care of that, I wandered over to Ellin's office where she was having a talk with Reg. Apparently, he was trying to make amends for the psychic telethon.

"Ellin, you're going to love this. We have a new sponsor. Tru-Flavor Flavored Waters. They came on board yesterday. They can help us stay afloat." He gave a nervous laugh. "On board. Waters. Afloat. Get it?"

Ellin gave Reg one of her laser beam stares. "How did this happen?"

Reg surprised me by asserting himself. "I called them. I checked with Candle De-Lite, too, and they agreed to stay on with us, as well."

He got another stare. I was surprised his clothes weren't smoldering.

"You have my cell phone number," she said. "You should have called me."

"You told me never to call you."

"That's because you're always pushing your wild ideas."

Assertive Reg was on a roll. "If you'd give me more responsibility, you'd see what I can do."

"I know what you can do, Reg. That's why you're still our warm up man."

"At least listen to my ideas before you shoot them down. I have good ideas."

Ellin paused. "Tell me one good idea."

Reg gulped and straightened his tie. "Now?"

"You said you had good ideas. Let's hear one."

"Well, um."

Come on, Reg, I thought. Don't cave now. This is probably your one chance.

"I, uh, think we ought to ask our viewers to call in and tell us their favorite guests," he said.

Ellin didn't say anything, so Reg felt brave enough to continue.

"You know, if they liked the pet psychic best, or the Tarot card reader. We could have a top ten, maybe have people vote for their favorite. Call in shows are popular. People could even vote on our website."

She didn't change her expression. "That's not bad."

Reg wilted with relief. "It's not?"

"It would be a good way to see what the public likes. We could possibly tailor a show towards favorite guests. Let's say the Tarot card reader is the number one choice. We could develop a show around the Tarot."

Reg brightened. "We could call it *It's In The Cards*."

She gave him a slight nod. "Okay. Start working on a top ten show—and leave the rest of the running of the PSN to me."

"Yes, of course. Thanks, Ellin! You won't be sorry."

He dashed out.

"Of course I'll be sorry," she said. "But it'll keep him out of my business."

"That was nice of you to encourage him," I said. "Are you mellowing?"

She cut her eyes at me. "Don't push it, Randall."

"You've got to feel better about the sponsors."

"Yes, I do."

I knew this sweet little moment couldn't last. She was still scheming.

"Now, what exactly is going on at the theater?" she asked.

"Oh, it's just some dead girl who likes to dance," I said.

She gave me the cold eye. "I swear, if one more ghost tries to take Cam over, I am going to scream."

"We think she's harmless."

"Then why is she here? You know as well as I do these ghosts have to have a reason. They can't just stay dead. What does she want?"

"She wants to dance."

"With Cam? I don't think so."

"Well, maybe if you'd dance with him, she wouldn't be here."

She gave a short mirthless laugh. "That won't work, Randall. She's probably after blood, or our first born. What are you doing about it?"

I didn't have a good answer for Ellin, which didn't matter, as she continued.

"It's a given I can't deal with spirits. They never show themselves to me. Cam gets all caught up in their sad stories—you know how he is. You'd better make sure this thing doesn't hurt him or Elise."

"Camden says she's friendly."

"I still don't like it."

Camden came in with Elise, who beamed at the sight of her mother and held out her arms. Ellin softened immediately.

"There's my baby. Come here, sweetie." She hugged Elise and cradled her in her arms. "Cam, would you like to explain about this dead dancing girl?"

Camden's glance to me said, thanks a lot. "There's a ghost in the old ballroom behind the stage. I'm trying to find out what she wants."

"You shouldn't be anywhere near a ghost. You know how you are."

"She's really very nice, as spirits go," he said. "She must have been too young to go to the ball, so now she's dancing there."

"It's not a good idea for you to get involved."

He changed the subject. "Reg told me about the new sponsor. So everything's settled?"

"For now. We still need to finish our discussion about Elise."

"As far as I'm concerned, that discussion is finished."

Elise made rude noises with her tongue.

"Enough already," I translated.

They kissed again while Elise and I exchanged a look. *Love, Dave,* came her little voice in my head.

I know, I thought back to her. "Ellin, is Diamond here?"

"She's down the hall."

"Still on the phone a lot?"

"Every time I've seen her on break, she's got that cell phone glued to her ear."

"Let me borrow Camden for a minute."

Camden and I went down a short hallway to a room that had been set up with a few cubicles for the psychics on call, Diamond and three women on loan from the Horoscopes division of the Psychic Service. Apparently no one needed psychic advice this afternoon. The three women had pulled their chairs together in one cubicle and were busy filing their fingernails and exchanging gossip. Diamond was alone in her cubicle reading a magazine.

"See if she'll swap Sherry stories with you," I said to Camden. "I want to know who she's been calling. If you can get her away from her desk that would be even better."

I waited out of sight in the hallway while he introduced himself. I wasn't sure how well Diamond would react to her replacement, but like most women, she liked what she saw. I could hear it in the way she spoke to him.

"Oh, so you're Sherry's new psychic," she said. "I've heard about you."

"Only temporary," Camden said.

Diamond gave an inelegant snort. "Oh, I know why. She's impossible, isn't she?"

"She can be a little intense."

"I'll bet she's told you all sorts of lies about me."

"No, she was very upset when you left."

"So upset she ran right out and hired you."

Camden asked the question I'd been wondering about. "Do you want to go back?"

"Not in a million years. This job suits me fine, and it's temporary, too. I have a very promising offer from another talented performer."

"That's great. Anyone I might know?"

"It's still in the planning stages."

"But you like it here at the PSN?" he asked.

"Yes, I do. I feel I'm really appreciated. Your wife runs this, doesn't she? What does she think about you and Sherry White?"

"She's happy I have a job."

Diamond actually laughed. "Being psychic makes things challenging, doesn't it? Normal jobs just aren't our thing."

"Sometimes it can be difficult."

"Why aren't you working here?" she asked. "Seems like this would be perfect for you."

"I'm a stay at home dad," Camden said. "And speaking of challenges, I have a psychic baby girl."

This caught her interest. "You're kidding. When did you find out?"

"Oh, I knew it before she was born. I'd love for you to see her. Do you have a moment?"

"Yes, I could take a break now."

As Camden and Diamond went down the hall, Diamond was saying, "You know, my powers manifested when I was just six."

Everyone at the PSN knows me, so after a friendly greeting, the three women went back to their conversation and paid me no attention. I stepped into Diamond's cubicle. A touchtone phone and computer were on the desk, along with the magazine she'd been reading, a calendar, and some sticky notes. Her pocketbook was on the floor. I searched through it and found her cell phone. I was delighted to find she wasn't using a passcode to unlock her phone. I guess she was so psychic she could tell if anyone was messing with it. I took a quick look at her recent calls and took photos of the numbers. I was out and down the hall long before Diamond returned. Then I made my way back to the main studio. Ellin was checking with the cameraman, and Camden and Elise were ready to go.

"Elise, you just created your first diversion," I said. "You are now officially a member of the Randall Detective Agency."

"Did you find anything?" Camden asked.

"Diamond calls one number more than any other. I'm going to find out who she's been talking to."

I didn't have to work very hard to find the answer. When we got home and I went into my office, the same number was written on my notepad, a number I'd jotted down so I could keep someone apprised of the Sherry White situation.

Mitch Stratton.

The other number she called the most? A number I'd recently put into my own phone.

Tony Kenner's.

# CHAPTER EIGHTEEN

*"Dancing in Circles"*

Back at the house Kary handed me a long list.

"Songs written from 1900 to 1912," she said.

"Thanks," I said. "Come help me look. Lindsey tells me if I can find the title of the song, the dancer can leave the ballroom."

We sat down on the floor in front of my CD collection and started hunting through the titles, searching for dates. It wasn't going to be easy. Most of the ragtime music I owned was written from 1900 to 1920. I knew the little dancer's tune wasn't anything by Scott Joplin, James Scott, or Joseph Lamb, the three main composers of ragtime, so we could eliminate those CDs. I thought her music might be "That Mysterious Rag," written in 1911, but when I played that CD, it wasn't the same song. It wasn't "Joy Rag," 1911, "Floating Along," 1906, "Invitation Rag," 1911, or "Midnight Rag," 1912, all tunes I thought she would choose.

Camden set another stack of CDs aside. "Maybe her tune has 'dance' in the title."

"Do you know how many songs of the ragtime era have 'dance'

in the title?" I asked.

"I'm guessing thousands?"

"Yes, and I don't have them all." I had "The Jazz Dance," "Oh! How She Can Dance," "Flower Dance," "I Want to Learn to Dance," and, of course, "The Ragtime Dance." None of these were little dancer's tune. "And somehow I don't think 'When Jennie Does That Low Down Dance' is what we're looking for," I said.

"Oo, play that one," Kary said.

We looked until dinnertime, when, to our happy surprise, Ellin brought home Baxter's barbecue sandwiches for everyone. Kary and I were glad to abandon our search and sink our teeth into the tangy goodness that is a Baxter's sandwich. With everyone around the table, the windows open to let in the warm summer breeze, the smell of barbecue, and the chirping of the birds, it was as if 302 Grace Street was doing its best to make us stay.

I get the message, I thought. No need to pile it on. I've got a few more days to find a solution to Kary's job situation.

Denny swept in, scooped up a sandwich, thanked Ellin profusely, and swept out again, saying something about having to rehearse his big number.

Ellin had Elise in one arm as the baby gulped down her evening bottle. "What's the latest on the ghost dancer? Would that be something to feature on the PSN?"

I handed Kary a pile of extra napkins and reached for more fries. "Two problems there," I said. "First, I don't think she'd show up on film, and second, she's tied to the ballroom. If I can find out the name of the song she's dancing to, she can move on."

I didn't mention that Lindsey had given me this assignment. Elise turned her head to give me the full power of her big blue eyes. For a moment, I thought I saw complete sympathy and understanding. Then she let out a very large burp that made everyone laugh.

"Thank you for your succinct comment on the situation," I said.

Ellin put the baby over her shoulder and patted her back. "She gets that from her father."

"I am so proud," Camden said.

Ellin had another concern. "What about Sherry White's threatening letters? Any ideas on that?"

"I think Sherry and Tony Kenner have created a big publicity stunt," I said. "Denny helped me set a trap, and tomorrow we'll see if he walked into it."

After supper, Ellin took Elise upstairs, and once more, Camden and Kary joined the search for the ghost dancer's song until all our eyes were crossing.

"You can't tell what it is?" Kary asked Camden as we eliminated yet another rag.

He shook his head. "My knowledge of ragtime music isn't as vast as Randall's. I can tell Joplin when I hear it, but that's my limit."

"You are so useless," I said.

Kary took the CD out of the player. "Why won't the dancer tell you?"

"It's a game for her. She's very young. Sixteen, maybe, or even younger."

Even though I was pretty sure her tune wasn't "Haunting Rag," written in 1911, we listened to it to make sure. I found a cute little number called "Peaches and Cream," written in 1905, that would have suited the dancer, but that wasn't her tune.

Then Kary brought up another problem. "Are you certain this song is from 1900 to 1912? Maybe it goes further back."

"It can't go too far back. It's definitely ragtime, and ragtime became popular right at the turn of the Twentieth Century." I pushed the stack of CDs aside. "That's enough for today."

We decided the proper antidote to our search was *The Giant Spider Invasion.* By the time the spider, part Styrofoam, part pipe cleaner toy gone horribly awry, put in an appearance behind screaming crowds of extras, we were all half asleep.

Camden turned off the TV. "Not as good as *The Killer Shrews.*"

"You got that right." I heaved myself out of the blue arm chair and nudged Kary, who was dozing in her rocking chair. "The giant spider has destroyed the city. Time for bed."

She yawned. "That's the most romantic thing you've ever said."

\*\*\*

I could hardly wait until Friday morning to see if Sherry's pet reporter bought the fake scoop. As soon as Camden secured Elise in her stroller, we walked over to Food Row to the convenience store on the corner, and I bought a *Galaxy*. The cover trumpeted a two-thousand pound woman giving birth to fifty-pound triplets, and a wolf boy marrying an alligator girl.

"This is too complicated for me," Camden said.

I searched through the gaudy pages. "Here we go. 'Stalked Songstress Threatened With Disfiguring Death.'" The article showed a picture of Sherry singing, her face screwed into an emotional tangle. "Looks like it's already happened." I read the article aloud. "'Besieged songbird Sherry White continues to be threatened by anonymous letters. The latest threatens to rip out her larynx with a claw hammer.' My words exactly. Kenner must have stopped the presses to get it in on time. Plus I am impressed by his use of 'besieged.'" I read on. "'Miss White declares to go on despite these horrendous threats. "Nothing can keep me from my public and my wonderful fans," she told the *Galaxy*. "They're all I have. I dedicate my life and my voice to them."' Excellent." I closed the paper. "Let's go see what her majesty has to say."

***

Camden and I found Sherry White in her dressing room, attempting to pull a comb through her orange curls. I had the *Galaxy* folded under my arm. "I read an interesting article in the *Galaxy* today," I said.

She yanked at her hair. "A disgusting little rag. I never read the tabloids."

"But a lot of your fans do, and if they read one of the latest issues, they would've known that the last letter you received referred to you as a heartless bitch."

"So?"

"So I'm wondering how the *Galaxy* knew the contents of a letter you shredded right in front of me. I'm also wondering why all the other letters were conveniently burned."

She kept tugging on her comb.

I came up and leaned against the dressing table. "You know, when everyone in the free world is a suspect, maybe the answer is nobody is a suspect."

She didn't look at me. "I don't know what you mean."

"Well, allow me to explain. Not long ago, Sherry White, Incorporated, was in a pretty bad slump. Seems all the other divas' albums were doing fine, but yours was limping along. What better way to drum up a little publicity and sympathy than to suddenly be stalked? You could go on all the talk shows and show everyone how brave you were. Yes, the show will go on! No one stops Sherry White, not even a slimy poison pen writer." I paused for a moment, but she didn't say anything. "You know, I've actually seen some of your movies, and I have to say, you're a decent actress."

She reacted to this criticism with a glare. "Decent!"

"Good enough to pull this off, anyway. A real newspaper would demand facts, but tabloids live on conjecture and fantasy. Perfect. So you leaked a few items to Tony Kenner."

She didn't answer.

"Okay," I said. "How about this? I gave Kenner a call. I told him you'd gotten another letter, one that mentioned throat surgery with a claw hammer." No need to tell her about Denny's uncanny impersonation of her voice. I held out the *Galaxy*, page folded back to the article. "Take a look."

She looked. Her tiny eyes narrowed. "How descriptive."

"Tell me the truth. You've been writing the letters, haven't you?"

"You're dismissed," she said. "Your services are no longer required."

"Case closed? Great. Camden and I will be on our way."

She grasped my arm. "You can't take Cam with you."

"How else is he going to get home?"

"I need him!"

"Then you'd better start being honest with me," I said. "Did you write the letters? Is this a publicity stunt?"

She let go of my arm and pushed it away. "No."

I didn't believe her. I tried something else. "Diamond has been calling Mitch Stratton constantly since she left."

She didn't even blink. "Telling him what a horrible monster I am, I'm sure."

"Why would she call Mitch?"

"Who knows why she does the things she does?"

"There may be a very good reason she's calling him," I said. "The two of them have something in common. They both feel betrayed."

"Betrayed?"

"How did Mitch feel when you took over Crystal Films?"

This time she did blink. "What does that have to do with anything? Crystal Films lost money and had to fold. I simply recreated the company and made it profitable."

"Did you discuss this with him?"

"No. We were divorced by then. He had to give the company to me. I saved him from bankruptcy. If anything, he should be grateful to me. And if he isn't, who cares?"

"What about Images? Does Mitch know you bought him out and changed the website to Visions? Ruining Mitch's companies seems to be a hobby of yours. Your makeover is dangerously close to plagiarism, I might add."

"I don't see how any of this is your business!"

"So this whole scheme is just you and Kenner? Diamond has nothing to do with it. Mitch has nothing to do with it. You hired me to solve this problem. Problem solved."

She reared back, and I expected to see flames shoot from her nostrils. "I've heard enough of this! Get out!"

"Sherry," Camden said. "We're trying to help you."

"The only way you can help me is to assure me my concerts will be perfect."

"If you'll just let Randall find out the—"

"Both of you just go!"

"Okay," I said. "You let me know when you're ready to talk."

"Out!"

"She didn't seem surprised about Diamond and Stratton," I said to Camden as we walked down the hallway. "You'd think she'd jump at the chance to blame the letters on them."

"If she's responsible for the letters, why did she hire you?"

"Well, it gives her scam validity."

"'Validity.' Nice one."

"It would've looked odd if she refused my offer," I said. "What besieged songbird wouldn't want my help?"

"She must have known you'd find the truth."

"No, I think she had it all figured out from the beginning. She fired her manager and agent so they wouldn't be around when she started the letters. She used her temper tantrums to keep everyone else at bay. Then she demanded more security and hired a private investigator, all to make her story look good."

"What I don't understand is why Kenner hasn't exposed her," Camden said. "It would be a huge story."

"But it would kill the golden goose. She must be paying him a fortune."

Elise, snug in her little front pack, had slept through Sherry's tirade and now yawned and opened her eyes. *Hungry,* she announced.

"I'd better find a couple of bottles," Camden said.

"All right," I said. "I'll drop you two off at home, and then I need to have a word with Diamond."

\*\*\*

At the PSN Diamond looked up from her computer keyboard.

"Oh, hello," she said. "What are you doing here?"

"Thought I'd check and see how you were doing."

She turned around in her chair. "That's very nice of you. I like it here. Of course, I don't plan to make this my career, but it's okay for now."

"Glad to hear it," I said. "So Sherry hasn't contacted you?"

"No. But I met her new psychic advisor. I wanted to hate him, but he's very nice. His wife's my boss, but you probably know that."

"Yeah, I've met her." And if you were truly psychic, you would've already divined that we all live together—in a manner of speaking. "Don't let me keep you from your work."

She shrugged. "No problem. It's kind of slow right now. Has Sherry gotten any more letters?"

"Yes, she has." I still had my copy of the *Galaxy*. "Take a look." Diamond's little nose wrinkled as she read the article. "You may have seen Tony Kenner backstage. He's a thin weasely guy."

"I know who Kenner is. I've heard Sherry talking to him, telling him her whole sad life story." She handed the paper back to me. "I wouldn't be surprised if they had some sort of arrangement."

"I'm surprised he never asked you for some dirt."

"Oh, he has. He's called me several times. I told him whatever dirt there is has already been uncovered. The world knows all about her."

"So you don't think these letters are anything to be worried about."

She sat back in her chair. "I think the letters are giving Sherry all the publicity her little black heart deserves. I don't think there's anything she doesn't want public."

"I need to know more about Mitch Stratton," I said.

Finally, a reaction. Her eyebrows lifted. "Why is that?"

"When we spoke earlier at the hotel, you said you knew him and that he was a nice guy."

"He is. He'd never send threatening letters to anyone."

"When's the last time you spoke to him?"

"Well, actually, that would be today."

I kept my expression neutral and waited for her to explain.

"We're just good friends. I told him I'd left Sherry, and he said he's going to take me on as his personal psychic. He likes to call for advice."

Or to find out what Sherry's up to.

"So he's in town?" I asked.

"He has family in Virginia. Sweetbriar."

A town about an hour or less from Parkland.

"He really appreciates me," Diamond continued, "Not like Sherry. I can assure you he's not behind the letters. I would've sensed something like that."

Oh, really? "What do you know about Crystal Films?"

"Don't you mean Crystal Clear?" she said. "That was my idea, the name, I mean. It came to me in a dream. Sherry White. Crystal Clear. It works. That's what she calls her smaller production company."

"But it was Crystal Films before, right?"

"Yes, but she wanted something new. She told me she wanted a name for her multimedia company, and that's what I came up with —not that I ever received any credit. Most of the best titles for her songs were my idea, too. She never would've thought of 'Angel of Love' on her own. That's why she needs me, even if she doesn't think she does. Can her new psychic come up with song titles? Probably not."

I decided not to mention that Camden was an excellent singer and could probably write songs if he wanted to.

Diamond shrugged again. "But that's her problem."

"You knew Mitch was an actor before he became a film maker."

"Yes. He said he preferred being behind the camera."

"He was in a Crystal Film movie," I said. "Did Sherry ever discuss this with you?"

"No. That must have been before I came to work for her."

"Were the Crystal Clear productions successful?"

"They did pretty well. There was a very nice Christmas special and one with some ice skating stars. Two movies were sold to the Hallmark Channel. Sherry wanted to diversify and go into TV, but the one pilot she did wasn't sold. If she'd listened to me, I could've saved her a lot of trouble and money. I knew the world wasn't ready for another Single Woman on the Town sitcom."

"Is Sherry still interested in TV?" I asked.

"I suppose. But she won't get anywhere without my advice."

"What about Images, Mitch's other company?" I asked. "I understand it's gone under."

"I'll bet you a million dollars Sherry's behind that," Diamond said. "I'm almost certain that's why Mitch had to come back to the states."

"Does she hate Mitch that much?"

"I think she's just trying to prove she's right about everything and he's wrong." Her desk phone rang. "I'd better get back to work."

I thanked her for her help, still not completely convinced she wasn't involved in the threatening letter scheme.

# CHAPTER NINETEEN

## *"I'm Still Dancin' With You"*

Kary had made peanut butter and banana sandwiches for lunch. Camden and Elise were upstairs taking a nap. I brought the bag of chips, and we ate on the porch. I told Kary my plan to use Denny's voice had worked, and Kenner had taken the bait.

"And Sherry gave a furious performance of denial."

"Sounds like she's really desperate," she said. "So you've eliminated Diamond and Mitch Stratton?"

"Just a couple of things to clear up."

After lunch, I called Patricia Lansdale again. This time she answered.

"So sorry I haven't gotten back to you, Mr. Randall. I've been very busy with my new act."

"No problem, Ms. Lansdale," I said. I wanted Kary to hear the conversation, so I asked, "Would you mind if I put you on speaker?"

"That's perfectly all right."

"Thanks," I said. "Sounds as if the Marigold breakup worked

out for you."

"Oh, yes," she said. "I didn't see it at first, but it was the best thing that could've happened. If I'd stayed as a Marigold, I never would've gone out on my own. I would've been a backup singer all my life. Today, I'm the star of the Tampa Midnight Club. I may not be as well-known as Sherry White, but I have my own fragrance, my own line of jewelry, and I put out a new CD every spring. When Sherry decided to leave the Marigolds, I was furious, but as everything's worked out really well for me, I'd have to say she did me a huge favor."

"Have you talked with her recently?" I asked.

"No, our friendship didn't survive the breakup. I haven't talked with her or seen her since then, except when I happen to hear something about her on the news, her new CD, a concert tour, things like that. All this business with threatening letters."

"What's your take on that?"

"There are a lot of crazy people out there," she said. "I guess Sherry's paying the price for being so famous. Sometimes fans can really get carried away. At the height of our fame, our fans were rabid."

"Anything the Marigolds did that might be considered scandalous?" I asked.

"I remember Sherry did a risqué photo shoot for *Elite Glamour*. Everyone's seen her bust. But that's not scandalous compared to today's standards. We partied hard and poor Tracey got into drugs."

"One of my other sources mentioned Jason Frost's parties."

There was a brief silence at the other end of the line. "Frost. Now there's a name I do remember. The parties at his studio were legendary."

"I understand there were some movies made of those parties."

She laughed. "Well, not exactly movies. Little films of ourselves dancing around. One of Sherry's boyfriends was going to use the footage for a documentary about the Marigolds, but nothing ever came of it."

And which one of Sherry's boyfriends became a film maker—excuse me, visual designer—with his own production company? Someone who parted on less than amiable terms, as he said?

In the background I heard someone call to her. "Mr. Randall, you'll have to excuse me, but I'm due at the theater in about half an hour. Was there anything else?"

"Ms. Lansdale, you wouldn't happen to have one of those little movies, would you?" I asked. "That would be a real bonus for my article."

"You know, I believe I might," she said. "Give me your email address. If I find it, I'll send you a copy."

I thanked her and ended the call. "I wonder if Sherry kept copies of those movies. There could be some interesting stuff."

Movement on the porch made me glance out the window. At first, I thought it was Lily, a vaguely female shape in a wide overcoat and a floppy hat pulled down low. But this figure was too tall to be Lily. I caught a glimpse of orange curl.

"Kary, looks like Sherry White's come to call."

We both hopped up and hurried to the door. When I opened it, Sherry pushed past us into the house. She didn't acknowledge Kary. I don't think she even saw her.

"You have to take care of this, Randall! Cam has to tell me everything will be all right." She took off her hat and the overcoat. She was so pale even her curls had lost their Day-Glo shine. She clutched a large yellow envelope.

"Your latest missive?" I asked.

"I didn't write this."

"Come have a seat."

She followed me into the island and stopped short. When he wasn't rehearsing at the theater, Denny spent most of his days either at the Pyramid or at Lily's, but at the moment, he was sitting on the sofa, painting his fingernails. When he saw my guest, he leaped up.

"Oh, my God! Sherry White! I don't believe it! I'm your biggest fan!"

"Sherry, this is Denny Kowalski."

Denny hopped from one foot to the other in delight. "This is so exciting! I do you!"

Sherry drew back. "Do me?"

"In my act. Wait right there; I'll show you."

"Not now, Denny," I said.

He was halfway up the stairs. "It'll only take a minute."

Sherry gave Kary a suspicious glance. "Who's this?"

"My associate, Kary Ingram."

"Can she be trusted?"

"Yes, of course, Ms. White," Kary said. "I'll be discreet, and I'll be happy to help you any way I can."

She looked around anxiously. "Where's Cam?"

"He's upstairs with Elise," I said. "What's the trouble? Another letter?" I didn't add, "That you wrote?"

Her voice trembled. "Something much worse."

She handed me the yellow envelope. Inside was a typed letter. Sherry was to cancel her tour, beginning with the Saturday concert, or the enclosed picture would be sent to the major newspapers. The picture was a black and white photograph of a nude, much younger Sherry clutching an equally nude teenage girl.

"Oh, my God," Kary said in an undertone.

Sherry moaned. "If this gets out, I'm ruined. The CGA will pull out all money and support. Zing Cola, Highlight Hair Care, everyone."

"CGA?" I asked.

"Christian Girls Alliance. They're even more wholesome than the Girl Scouts. I'm their spokesperson."

"There wasn't a demand for money?"

"No, just to cancel the tour. I don't understand!"

"How old is this girl?" I asked.

Sherry wouldn't look at the picture. "I don't know."

"Who is she? When was this taken?"

"I don't remember."

"What, there were so many?"

Up came her head, her tiny eyes glaring. "I'll admit it was stupid, but I never did it again."

"This is certainly a step up from those letters," I said.

"You idiot, I didn't do this!" She began to shake. "Oh, my God, my new CD! What a farce. 'Love, Youth, and Beauty.' No, this can't be happening! It's too horrible." She let Kary put her arm around her shoulders.

"Sherry, we'll help you." Kary said.

I looked at the photo again. It was high quality, printed on glossy paper. Sherry's little eyes were closed. The young girl's head was snuggled into the mass of Sherry's curls. I couldn't see her face, just her naked back and dark hair tied in a ponytail. There was something else about the picture, something I'd seen before, but I couldn't quite figure out what it was.

Sherry was still shaking and moaning. "Randall, you have to take care of this."

"Only if you tell me the truth from now on," I said. "Did you send those letters to yourself?"

She pulled away from Kary. "Yes, yes, I admit it, but I had nothing to do with this dreadful picture! You have to do something."

"Explain about the picture."

"I don't remember! I was a celebrity. People took my picture everywhere I went!"

"You weren't naked everywhere you went."

She glared. "It must have been at a nightclub. I think we'd all had too much to drink."

"You mean, the kid was drunk, too?"

She had the grace to look ashamed. "I suppose so. I don't remember."

Camden must have sensed something was wrong because he came down the stairs, his expression concerned. "What's happened?"

I handed him the picture. "This."

He winced. "This isn't the only copy."

I thought Sherry was going to faint. "No!"

"Can you tell where the other copies are?" I asked Camden.

He shook his head. "I can't tell. It's Sherry again." He gave her a sympathetic glance. "You're so upset, your vibes are everywhere."

I looked at the picture again and realized what I'd missed before. The way the girl was positioned made it hard to see, but if I wasn't mistaken, there was a tattoo on her arm, the faintest shadow of a twisting rose vine peeking out from under her elbow. "This girl is Diamond."

He carefully touched the image. "Yes."

"A very young Diamond."

"She was sixteen."

A look of revulsion crossed Sherry's face. "Diamond? How could that be? You're wrong! You have to be wrong!"

"Yoo-hoo!" Denny sang out as he flounced in, orange wig bouncing with Sherry's trademark curls. "Here she is, your angel of love, Miss Sherry White!"

Sherry's mouth hung open as Denny paraded around the island, singing a credible imitation of her shrieking soprano. With his long face and the wig, he looked exactly like her, only taller and possibly a touch more feminine.

We had to wait until Denny finished a chorus of "Angel of Love." Sherry was too stunned to speak, but she didn't have to tell me who the photographer was. Down in the corner of the picture was a symbol, a stylized "J" and "F."

Jason Frost.

\*\*\*

Camden, Kary, and Denny stayed to console Sherry while I took the photo to Frost's house. He greeted me at the front door and invited me in.

"What can I do for you today, Randall?"

I showed him the picture. "Recognize this?"

He went as pale as Sherry. He snatched the picture from me. "Where did you get that?"

"Did you take this picture?"

The photograph flapped in his trembling hand. "This is terrible. Where did you get this? How can this be? I gave this to Sherry." He shoved it back at me.

"Start at the beginning and explain," I said.

He sank into one of the chairs in the foyer. "When I first

started out, I took photos for art magazines. Nudes, sometimes, of course, but nothing vulgar. Sherry White was new on the scene, and *Celebrity* wanted some nice artsy shots, so they called me. I was thrilled by the opportunity, maybe too thrilled. We all had too much to drink and started fooling around, but, my God, how did this happen? I took only a few of them nude and gave the pictures to Sherry."

"Who's the girl?" I asked, to see if he could confirm it was Diamond.

"I don't know if she ever gave her name."

"How old was she?"

"The agency wouldn't have sent someone underage!"

"What agency?"

"I'd have to look it up. It was at least twelve years ago."

"If you didn't send this, the girl could have stolen them."

"But what could she want after all this time? Why ruin Sherry's career now?"

"Have you talked with Sherry lately?" I asked. "She isn't likely to win any popularity contests."

"Yes, but this—this is beyond revenge. This is sick." He looked at the rows of children's pictures and then to me with pleading eyes. "Never mind about Sherry's career. If this gets out, *I'll* be ruined. I'm known for my pictures of children, Randall. Children!"

"Who else would have been in your studio?" I asked.

"No one!"

"You didn't have any assistants? Anyone just hanging around?"

"I can't remember. I used to have photography students, but only a few. Oh, my God." He put his head down in his hands.

I took out my phone. "What was the name of the modeling agency?"

"I'm trying to think. Super something. Super Creations. I worked with them all the time. They wouldn't have sent an under-age girl."

Online, I found Super Creations with offices in New York and Los Angeles. The company was proud of their models and conveniently listed them. Jason said the infamous photo shoot was twelve years ago, so I checked the list from that year. During that time period, the listing of models employed by Super Creations included an Angelina Diamonte.

It was Diamond, all right.

Frost raised his head. "She must have lied about her age. You have to believe me. Someone is trying to destroy my career."

"I think someone is trying to destroy Sherry's career, and you got caught in the middle," I said. "The photo was sent to her, not you. I'm pretty sure this is Diamond's way of getting back at Sherry."

"Then stop her," he said. "Do whatever it takes."

# CHAPTER TWENTY

## *"I'm Happy Just to Dance With You"*

When I got back to the house, Camden, Kary, and Denny were still trying to comfort Sherry. She jumped to her feet and pushed her hair back. Curls sprang in all directions.

"What did he say? Did he do this? Cam, did you see anything? What am I going to do? I have to find Diamond! If she's responsible, I'll sue her for everything she's got."

"And have this picture come to light?" I said. "Maybe not the smartest move."

"What did Jason say? He had to know something."

"He's just as upset as you are."

"Well, that's impossible."

"I did find out that Diamond's real name is Angelina Diamonte, and I think she lied about her age to the modeling agency," I said. "A few years later, she decided to become psychic and lend her services to the famous Sherry White. So she had access to everything in your home, right? She probably found the pictures, and when her life with you didn't work out, she resulted to blackmail."

Sherry choked. "But she couldn't have!"

"Jason Frost gave the pictures to you, right? Just the three of you late one evening. Just a few extra fun shots."

I thought Sherry was going to stop breathing. "No, that's impossible! I threw those pictures away!" She finally managed to gasp. "I—I thought I did. Diamond!" Her features hardened and she spoke through clenched teeth. "After all I did for her!"

"What exactly did you do for her?" I asked.

"I gave her everything. She toured with me, rode in the limos, the private jet, had the best hotels, the gourmet meals, clothes, jewelry, whatever she wanted."

"Did you love her?"

"Of course not! I needed her psychic advice, so naturally, I treated her well."

"Is it possible she loved you?"

"She never gave any indication that this was anything more than a business arrangement."

I took another look at the photo. The young girl's posture was one of complete and loving surrender. Maybe it had been all business for Sherry, but my guess was Diamond had been desperately in love with her idol from the beginning, rescued the photos from the trash to keep as treasured souvenirs, and when Sherry didn't respond, hell began to boil up a good case of scorned fury.

Sherry gazed at me with pleading eyes. "Are you going to be able to help me? Talk to her, see what can be done. If she has feelings for me, surely she won't ruin my career."

"I don't know," I said. "I'll do my best, but if she's this obsessed with you, then we may be looking at a case of 'if I can't have you, no one else will.'"

She sobbed. "What am I going to do?"

Denny patted her shoulder. "Sherry, I'm sure David has a plan."

She turned to Camden. "What should I do, Cam?"

"I think you should go on as you usually do," he said. "Rehearse your songs. Concentrate on your music and let Randall take care of this."

"And let me know if Kenner calls," I said.

Camden tried to convince her to go back to the auditorium. She insisted he come with her.

"Elise is still sleeping," he said. "Why don't you come hold her until she finishes her nap? If she wakes when you pick her up, you can rock her for a while. It'll calm you down."

"That sounds wonderful," she said.

Denny promised to fly to her side if she needed him. Camden showed her the way to his bedroom and then returned to the island.

"There's one other thing about that picture, Randall," he said. "A lot of darkness."

I was not happy to hear this. "Evil spirit darkness?"

"I'm afraid so, but it's not in Sherry."

"So it could be in Diamond," I said. "Or Jason Frost."

"Evil spirit darkness?" Denny said, alarmed.

"Long story," I said. "Let's just say whoever's after Sherry is not in full control."

My phone rang. It was Jake Banner. "Yo, Randall! Kenner just came into the *Galaxy* office. Now's your chance, bud."

"Thanks," I said. I ended the call. "Speaking of evil spirit darkness, there is finally a Kenner sighting."

\*\*\*

Things at the *Galaxy* office were hopping—literally. Someone's two-headed frog had escaped. Most people were screaming and trying to swat it, while others were using empty trashcans, boxes, and hats in attempts to catch the critter.

I made my way to the back where Jake Banner was sitting at his desk, feet up, enjoying the show. He pointed to Kenner, who gave me a furious glare.

"What the hell do you want?"

"Just stopped by to see Jake," I said. "You seem upset. Did Sherry White foil the great Tony Kenner? I hear you two have an excellent symbiotic relationship." I'd have to remember to tell Camden I had the opportunity to use "symbiotic." Too bad it was wasted on Kenner.

He scrunched up his face. "What do you mean by that?"

"She gives you all kinds of terrible things to say about her in the *Galaxy*."

"Ha! Even if she did, so what?"

"Well, for one thing, she's defrauding her fans," I said. "There's no real threat. Her life's not in danger."

His weasel eyes narrowed. "I don't need a lecture from you."

"If Sherry's not feeding you false information, who is?"

"I'm not revealing my sources."

"Sherry's your only source for these letters, and she's not going to give you any more dirt," I said.

"What makes you think I need her? She's not the only story in town."

"That's a good idea," I said. "Find other stories."

He pushed past me. "We're done."

As he stalked off, he kicked a trashcan and sent the two-headed frog airborne, causing a renewal of the screams and curses.

Jake chuckled. "You rattled him good, Randall."

"Think he'll back off?"

"Oh, yeah. He was already in a wad before you came. Seems somebody called saying they had dynamite info on Sherry and then never showed. He's pretty sure he's been double-crossed. Couldn't happen to a nicer guy."

Sherry, I thought, finally breaking it off with him.

"Any idea what that might have been about?" Jake asked.

"I believe I do," I said. "Thanks."

***

Camden, in a wild diversion from his usual lasagna, made meat loaf for supper, along with green beans and potatoes. Cindy and Oreo slid around my legs, hoping for a handout, but I ate every crumb.

After supper, Kary and I were in my office searching for the right ghostly song when I had a call from Patricia Lansdale.

"I found one of those movies," she said. "Someone must have transferred it for me from the old VHS tape to a DVD. It's not very much, maybe about ten minutes long. I've downloaded it and can send you a copy."

After about five minutes, I had the file. Kary pulled the client chair around to watch. The movie, as Patricia had said, was of a lot of people drinking and dancing around. Loud Marigold music drowned out any conversation.

"That's Sherry," I said. "I recognize the hair, and there's a younger yet still gloomy-looking Jason Frost."

Kary leaned forward for a closer look. "The two women in yellow dresses must be Tracey and Patricia."

Mitch must have set his camera on a tripod because there he was, shaking his hips with a young dark-haired woman. They danced in and out of frame, but I knew who she was and pointed her out to Kary.

"There's Angelina Diamonte, better known as Diamond. Sherry insisted she didn't know this girl, but here she is, dancing at one of Jason Frost's famous parties."

"Before or after the infamous nude picture?"

"A very good question and one I intend to ask Diamond."

We searched a while longer, and then Kary went upstairs. I found a dirty coffee cup on my desk and took it into the kitchen. Since Camden had supported himself during his wandering years by washing dishes, it was odd to find dirty plates and a frying pan in the sink. With feeding Elise and taking naps when he could, as well as soothing Diva Sherry, I understood he was off his game.

As I reached for the dishwashing liquid and a sponge, Denny came around the corner from the dining room. "Oh, I'll get those, David. It's my turn."

I had to look twice to make sure it was Denny. He had on a man's dark brown suit and had pulled his long hair back into a ponytail. His tie had a wild pattern of dancing ducks, but otherwise, he looked like a he. I was so used to seeing him in a dress, his appearance was almost jarring.

"What's with the outfit?" I asked.

He grimaced. "My little Lily wanted to see what I'd look like, and the dear has gone through such a remarkable transformation for me, I couldn't say no to a simple change of clothes."

"It works."

"Thank you, but it's so drab. I miss my feathers and frills." He took off his jacket and rolled up his shirtsleeves. "Well, one night won't kill me. Pass me that sponge, would you?"

I let him take over the dishwashing. "You've done a lot for Lily. I've never seen her so happy and confident."

"She's done a lot for me, too. She's so sweet and kind. Someone uncomplicated is exactly what I need." He scrubbed the spatula. "We may be talking serious relationship here, David."

"Would you go so far as to call her your soul mate?"

He paused in his scrubbing. "I believe I would."

"Congratulations."

Denny frowned at the rim of burned cheese on the frying pan. "It's such a shame Sherry was never able to find someone. She went through scores of lovers before she met Mitch Stratton. All her fans were certain that relationship was going to work out, but it didn't." He scrubbed harder. "No one understood why they split. It was obvious she adored him. They were obsessed with each other."

"Obsession never seems to work out," I said, thinking of Kary. I was willing to leave everything and follow her, but would being so selfless put a strain on our relationship? Emotions had a habit of sneaking up when you least expected them. Would Kary feel guilty? Would I feel resentful?

Denny set the clean pan aside and reached for a plate. "At least Lily doesn't have a color fetish like Sherry. Everyone knows yellow is her unlucky color."

"Because of the Marigolds."

"That's right. All they wore was yellow, yellow and orange. When Sherry broke away for her solo career, she vowed she'd never wear yellow again." He finished with the plate and dried his hands. "I understand the other two girls were angry with her for breaking up the act, so for Sherry, there would be all kinds of bad vibes associated with yellow. Poor Sherry. She doesn't have very many friends, does she? Can you find the person who sent that horrible picture?"

"I think so."

"You think it's that young woman, Diamond?"

"Looks that way."

Denny shook his head sadly. "People will do anything for love, won't they?"

I thought of the picture of Sherry and Diamond, of Diamond's blissful expression and her fierce embrace. "They sure will."

# CHAPTER TWENTY-ONE

### *"Last Dance"*

It was a busy Saturday morning with everyone heading out in all directions. One of Kary's teacher friends stopped by to say there was a possible opening at Dellwood Elementary in Parkland, so Kary went with her to check it out. Sherry didn't call demanding Camden, so he kept Elise while Ellin, as usual, charged to the PSN to keep Reg in line. I set about getting in touch with Diamond.

She was in her hotel room when I called.

"I knew you were going to call," she said.

"I knew you were going to have breakfast with me."

"That sounds great."

"I'll be by in about fifteen minutes."

Diamond, I thought, if you were truly psychic, you wouldn't have anything to do with me.

I met her in the lobby of the Mid-Town Hotel. She had on a yellow blouse and a short yellow skirt. Yellow. I might have known.

"Do you mind if we eat at the hotel?" she said. "They have a nice breakfast buffet." She looked up under long lashes. "And who knows where it may lead?"

Who knows, indeed.

The Mid-Town breakfast buffet stretched to the far corner of the dining hall. After piling our plates high, we sat down.

Diamond spread her napkin in her lap. "I have to admit I'm curious how things are going with Sherry."

"Oh, let's not talk about her," I said. "Let's talk about you. Have you always been psychic?"

"Oh, yes. My mother and grandmother were, too."

"A hard way to make a living, though."

"I don't think so."

"When I first met you, I thought you were an actress or a model."

"Oh?" She smiled and fluffed her hair. "Thanks. I did some modeling once. In New York."

I looked suitably impressed. "You must have had a great time there. Lots of friends, lots of parties."

"It was okay, but I got bored with it." She put down her fork. "Do you think Sherry would take me back?"

The question caught me off guard. "I thought you hated her. I thought she was impossible to work for."

"Yeah, well, you kinda get used to it." She took her time buttering a piece of toast and then said, "You, um, wouldn't put in a good word for me, would you?"

"I thought when Mitch got back from his travels he wanted you to be his psychic adviser."

"I've had some time to think things over. I think I can deal with Sherry now."

Still carrying that torch, eh? "What if she says no?"

"I've got a backup plan. I can be Mitch's advisor. Will you talk to her, see how she reacts to the idea?"

Violently, I imagine. "If that's what you want."

She gave me a thoughtful look, as if deciding what else to say. After a moment, she said, "Tell her I can help her with this situation."

"What situation?" I asked.

"I'm psychic. I know something else is going on."

"How about letting me in on it?"

She glanced around the room as if expecting to see reporters and TV cameras behind every table. She lowered her voice. "All right. Last night, I had a vision of Sherry receiving an envelope. I know what's inside that envelope. I also know that someone wants to use what's in the envelope to make her stop her concert tour. If she'll take me back, I can keep that from happening."

"Who wants to stop her tour?"

"That information is only for Sherry."

I did not believe for a second that Diamond had experienced a psychic vision. I had been wondering why the letter that came with the photo hadn't demanded any money. Now I knew. Diamond didn't want money. She wanted to be with Sherry, and this was her elaborate scheme to get back in her idol's good graces.

Wait a minute, I thought. Sherry wasn't the one who double-crossed Tony Kenner. I'll bet Diamond called him with this "dynamite info," and then realized she had a dynamite way to save Sherry's career. "What's in the envelope?"

"Something from Sherry's past. Something she needs to see."

"Then why not just give her a call?"

"She refuses to answer my calls."

"You think I can successfully plead your case?"

She leaned forward. "Tell her these exact words. 'I know who wants to destroy your career.' She'll believe you."

"What if she doesn't?" I said. This did not sound like evil spirit behavior. "You've gone out of your way to convince me that you hate the woman. Why this sudden change of heart? Why should you care what happens to Sherry or to her career?"

Diamond looked down at her plate. "I was angry and upset. I had to get out of there, have some time alone to think. I really want to go back. She needs me. She may not think she does, but she needs me."

No, I thought. It's the other way around. "Okay. I'll tell her, but I can't promise anything."

"Oh, she'll want to speak with me. Her career means everything to her." She gave me another look, this one full of promise. "Would you like to come up to my room?"

"That sounds nice." Because Camden had said there were copies, and that would give me the perfect opportunity to search for the photos. Maybe Diamond planned to give them to Sherry, but I couldn't take that chance. I'd promised to get them back.

In the elevator, she gave me a long kiss. She could hardly get her room door open fast enough. I needed to slow things way down.

"Tell you what," I said. "How about if you hop in the shower and I'll join you in a minute?"

She grinned and ran to the bathroom. As soon as I heard the water running, I began my search. I yanked open drawers and rooted through clothes, looked under the bed, behind the curtains, in the closet. Nothing. Damn, there were only so many places to hide things in a hotel room. Maybe she'd put the other photos in the safe downstairs. Maybe she'd given them to a friend. Maybe she'd swallowed them.

Her voice sang, "Oh, David."

"Be right there."

I looked behind the bureau and under the table and chairs, hoping to find an envelope taped beneath. Still nothing.

"David."

"Coming!"

I looked under the trashcan, in the trashcan, under the pillows and behind the sad-looking water color picture of some non-existent Italian villa. Now what?

"David?"

I felt under the mattress, hoping for the crackle of an envelope. I even stood on the bed and checked the overhead light fixture, a large, old-fashioned piece of glass with a scalloped edge. Nothing. Last places to check: the minifridge and the microwave. The photos weren't in the fridge or in the microwave, but as I closed the microwave door, I caught a glimpse of something. Underneath the microwave was just enough space for a manila envelope. I lifted the microwave, took the envelope, and looked inside. Bingo.

"David, I'm squeaky clean."

"I'll be right there," I said as I hurried out. She'd be squeaky clean, all right, and mad as hell. I hoped she'd be too mad to suspect I'd taken her blackmail material.

***

Sherry sobbed grateful tears. "I can't believe you found them. Are you sure this is all of them?"

Before meeting Sherry in her dressing room and handing over the envelope, I'd let Camden hold it. "Camden's sure. You can go on with your tour as planned."

She wiped her face. "I'm going to sue Diamond to the ends of the earth. How dare she try a stunt like this?"

"She was trying to get your attention," I said. "She wants to come back."

"There's no way in hell I'd have her back."

"Think about it, Sherry. You already know what she's like and what she's capable of. Wouldn't having her around be easier than hiring someone you don't know?"

"I thought Cam would come with me," she said.

"No. He can't leave his wife and baby, and he doesn't want to."

"I'll never take Diamond back. I'm calling the police and having her arrested." She shook the envelope. "This is proof!"

"Do you want anyone else to see that photograph?"

She stopped. "No."

"Then calm down and consider your options. Diamond was going to sell the photo to Tony Kenner so he could splash it all over the front page of the *Galaxy*, but she had a last minute change of heart. She decided she wanted to be the one who saved you. You can forgive Diamond and have a friend for life. You can find another psychic and hope he or she doesn't backstab you. Or you can call the police and have this sordid little escapade from your past all over the news."

She sat quietly for longer than I thought she could. Then she said, "Where's Diamond now?"

"Mid-Town Hotel. Room sixty-three. Wet and angry."

"I don't even want to know what that means." She picked up her cell phone from her dressing table. She called the hotel and asked for Diamond's room. Her expression changed. Her face paled. "What? Oh, my God. No, no, I'm not a relative. Never mind." She closed her phone. "Diamond's dead. They think she's been murdered." Her eyes were huge. "David, what did you do?"

My heart landed somewhere near my feet. "When she went into the bathroom to take a shower, I found the pictures and got out of there."

Sherry's voice trembled. "Then you were the last one to see her alive."

***

I left Sherry's dressing room and sat in the Fury for a long while, trying to decide what to do. If I went back to the Mid-Town Hotel, I'd run into Jordan Finley, and he'd know something was up. He might even see it as a case of the criminal returning to the scene of the crime. If Diamond had been murdered, then she'd told me the truth. Someone else wanted to use those photos to ruin Sherry. Tony Kenner, angry because she'd changed her mind? Boyfriend Mitch Stratton, whom I suspected wanted the pictures to get back at Sherry for destroying not only his acting career but both of his fledgling companies? Diamond must have gone back on her promise to sell him the photos, as well. Or was the murderer Jason Frost, frantic to protect his reputation?

Finally I decided my safest course of action was to go back to the hotel anyway and risk the wrath of Jordan.

Aside from the usual crush of police cars and emergency vehicles outside the Mid-Town, I was surprised to see a young officer holding Elise. Then I realized Jordan must have wanted Camden to have a look at the crime scene.

"Mr. Randall," the officer said. "Detective Finley will want to talk to you."

I took Elise, who gave me a welcoming burp. "I'm sure he will."

I didn't have to wait long before Jordan and Camden came out the front door. I handed him the baby. "You okay?"

He nodded. "I just need a minute." Elise snuggled in closer.

Jordan gave me a hard glare. "Glad you showed up, Randall. The desk clerk remembers seeing someone fitting your description visiting Ms. Diamonte before. She remembers seeing you today. The people in the dining room remember seeing you and Ms. Diamonte having breakfast. Guess it's the curse of being so dashing, eh?" He took out his phone to check his notes. "Round about eight thirty, the clerk recalls seeing the two of you at the elevator. Then she remembers seeing you leave shortly after, maybe fifteen minutes or so and returning fifteen minutes later. Then you came back downstairs around nine-thirty." His eyes narrowed. "Anything you'd like to tell me?"

"Nothing happened," I said. "Diamond wanted me to talk to Sherry to see if Sherry would take her back as her psychic. I said I would. I went upstairs with her around 8:30 and left at 8:45."

Jordan glanced at his notes again. "The clerk remembers seeing you return a few minutes later."

What was going on? "The clerk is mistaken. I didn't come back."

"The young woman was found on the bathroom floor as if she'd slipped and hit her head in the shower. You're sure you didn't join her?"

"She wanted me to, but I said no, thanks."

Jordan kept his skeptical expression. "She was in the shower when you left? You see anyone in the hallway? Know why anyone would want Ms. Diamonte dead?"

"No." If Jordan didn't know about the pictures, I wasn't going to tell him. Not yet. If there was a way to solve this without ruining

Sherry's career, I wanted to find it.

"She express any worries or concerns to you?" he asked.

"She wanted to get back with Sherry, that's all."

"Had she had any conversations with Miss White about this? Was there any possibility of Miss White rehiring her?"

"I don't know," I said.

"When Diamond heard someone knock, she thought it was Randall coming back," Camden said, "so she opened the door without looking first."

I turned to Jordan to make sure this was clear. "She thought it was me, but it wasn't."

"I heard him."

Camden arranged Elise in the crook of his elbow. "Whoever it was wanted something from her and was very angry when she didn't have it. Furiously angry. The waves of emotion filled that room."

Jordan frowned. "Now what would be so important?"

Like me, Camden didn't want to bring up the photos if there was any way to save Sherry's reputation. "It's usually money, isn't it?"

"Sherry White fired Ms. Diamonte," he said. "As I recall, this was not a pretty picture."

In more ways than one, I thought. "Sherry fires lots of people," I said. "If anything, Diamond would've wanted to kill her."

"It's possible she took something of Miss White's when she left, and Miss White wanted it back."

"Good grief, Jordan. Sherry White's rich enough to replace anything lost or stolen." Except incriminating photographs.

He was not convinced. "You never know with these superstars."

"You think Sherry killed her?"

"Or had her killed."

"It wasn't Sherry," Camden said. "Believe me, I'd recognize those vibrations."

"I need substantial evidence, Cam, you know that." Jordan said. "I'll go have a word with her. Randall, stay where I can reach you."

He gave Elise a little pat on her head and walked back to his squad car. Camden and Elise gave me identical deep looks. "What did Sherry do with the pictures?" Camden asked.

"If she has any sense, she destroyed them and won't mention them to Jordan." I let out the breath I'd been holding. "Man, I feel rotten. If I hadn't found the pictures, maybe Diamond would still be alive."

"No," Camden said. "The murderer would've killed her, anyway."

"You didn't get anything on the killer? Evil spirit darkness hanging around? I wouldn't put murder past Tony Kenner, but there's Stratton and Frost to consider, plus anyone Diamond alienated while she was with Sherry."

"There was plenty of darkness," he said. "Too dark for me to see much of anything. What do you want to do?"

I thought of Diamond's intense little face and the softer expression in the photograph. "I want to find who did this. Jason Frost told me to do whatever it takes to keep that photo out of the papers. Maybe he decided to do whatever it takes."

# CHAPTER TWENTY-TWO

### *"I Won't Dance"*

T hat's crazy," Frost said when we confronted him at his house. "I've been here all day. Besides, I had no idea that woman was at the Mid-Town Hotel, and even if I did know, how could I have gotten in to see her? She wouldn't have let me in."

"She might," I said. "She might have remembered all the good times at your parties."

"I don't remember her being at any of my parties."

"I've seen a little movie that proves otherwise." As he stared at me in disbelief, I said, "Patricia Lansdale sent me a copy. It shows Diamond dancing with Mitch Stratton while the Marigolds look on. You're in there, too, having a drink with Sherry."

Frost put both hands out, palms up as if pushing me away. "Look. You can't expect me to remember everyone who came to my parties. If you don't have any news about that photo, I'm going to have to ask you to leave."

"The photos have been destroyed," I said. "Your career is safe."

This had the effect of deflating Frost's anger. "Are you sure?"

"I took them to Sherry. She'll shred them to confetti, I promise." She'd better, I thought.

"Thank God." He looked puzzled. "Then why did someone kill Ms. Diamonte? If there are no photos, there's no chance of blackmailing anyone."

"I think losing that chance made someone very, very angry," I said.

"That someone is not me. The only thing I am is relieved."

Camden held out his hand. "Sorry, Jason. Randall has to follow every possible lead."

Frost shook his hand. "Yes, I understand, but to be accused of murder is not something I expected."

"I'm sure he'll be able to find whoever killed Diamond."

"I certainly hope so," Frost said.

"Me, too," I said as we returned to my car. I waited until Elise was safely strapped into her car seat. "I take it you didn't sense any dark murderous vibes?"

"Just relief, like he said."

"Okay, so we can eliminate Jason. What about Kenner? He was furious that one of his sources had gone back on a deal. I'm almost certain that source was Diamond, but did Kenner know it was Diamond? She probably didn't give him her real name."

"But Kenner looks nothing like you," Camden said. "The clerk said it was a tall dark-haired man. The only person who knows Diamond and fits that description is Mitch Stratton."

I thought about the phone call I'd had with Stratton. "Who was coming home to Sweetbriar, Virginia, which is only an hour away."

\*\*\*

We decided we needed food in order to continue pondering. Flip's was the closest, so we stopped by, ordered a couple of Flip burgers and fries, and sat at one of the picnic tables the little burger place provided. We'd finished our lunch and Elise had successfully levitated a French fry when the bright red Echo pulled up and Valerie Banner hopped out.

"Oh, my gosh, have you guys heard the news? That Diamond woman was killed. I heard someone say she was found in the shower. What if she was killed in the shower, just like that movie, *Psycho*! A Psychic Psycho! Can you believe it? What does it mean?"

"It means she's dead," I said.

"But why? Who'd want to kill her? I can see why people would want to kill Sherry, but what did this woman do? Remember how furious Sherry was when Diamond left her? Do you think Sherry killed her? Are you on this case, too, David? This is big, I mean, really big. Do you suppose the same person who's been sending the threatening letters is the murderer?"

"Have you talked to your Uncle Jake recently?" I asked.

This momentarily stopped the flow of excitement. "What's that got to do with this?"

"He can explain about the symbiotic relationship between Sherry and the tabloids."

"'Symbiotic,'" Camden said. "Excellent choice."

"Would you believe this is the second time I've been able to use it? It's been a while since I whipped out a ten-dollar word. I deserve double points."

Valerie jumped up and down. "But what about the *murder*? Do the police have any leads, any clues?"

"We don't know any more than you do, Valerie." I gathered all our trash and tossed it into a nearby trash can.

She stopped jumping. "Where are you going now?"

"Home."

"So you're not on this case?"

"No one has hired me to find Diamond's killer."

"But we could find the killer. I have some information that might crack this case wide open!"

"Okay, Nancy Drew. What've you got?"

She bristled a little at the nickname, but she was too excited about her clue to stay annoyed. "Will you let me help out?"

"I might."

"Cam, make him promise."

He wedged the last little bits of French fry out of Elise's fingers. "If things don't get too dangerous," he said.

"Oh, pooh. I'm ready for danger." She dug into her shoulder bag and brought out a piece of paper. "I have a clue."

"Sounds interesting," I said.

She clutched the paper to her chest. "This is my deal, David. I want to know what's going on."

"Tell me your clue and I might let you in on things."

"I talked with the clerk at the hotel. She has a complete description of the killer. She says he was tall, had dark hair, and was very good-looking."

"That's me, Valerie."

"Gosh, aren't we puffed up?"

"No, I mean, the clerk remembers seeing me when I went to talk to Diamond."

"Oh," she said. "Damn it." She wasn't down for long. "You went to talk to Diamond today? You were one of the last people to see her alive? Why did you want to talk to her again? Did she have some new info about the letters? She wrote them, right? So Sherry hired someone to take her out."

There was no way I was mentioning the photos to Valerie. "I wanted to know some background about her relationship with Sherry, that's all. She invited me up to her room, so I said yes."

Again, Valerie looked daunted. Again she said, "Oh."

The last thing I wanted was to involve Valerie. "Unless someone hires me to find Diamond's killer, I'm staying out of this and you will, too. Let the police find the murderer."

"But I want in on this story. I want to help solve this crime."

"Not this time."

She made several huffing noises and left.

"I suppose Sherry doesn't remember that Diamond attended Jason's parties. It was several years ago," Camden said.

"That's one of the questions I plan to ask her, and you're going to be holding her hand when I ask it."

"You'll get that chance sooner than you think."

My phone rang. It was Sherry, just on the verge of hysterics.

"That awful policeman just grilled me without any regard for my nerves! I'm completely shattered. I can't stay here. I'm too upset. Is Cam there? Would he mind if I came back to his house? The people here are devoid of sympathy!"

"He wouldn't mind," I said. "In fact, I have a few questions for you, too."

She made some sputtering noises and hung up.

"Sherry's on her way to 302 Grace," I said to Camden. "We'll see what she has to say about this."

\*\*\*

We were waiting on the porch when Sherry arrived in a taxi. She insisted on going inside and took a seat on the green corduroy sofa. She looked frayed and anxious, her orange curls in tight little springs.

"Cam, you know I had nothing to do with Diamond's death, but that dreadful policeman considers me a suspect!"

"He's only doing his job," Camden said. "He has to clear everyone who knew her."

"But it's a fact Diamond and I quarreled, and I was furious when she left." She gave me a glare. "I don't know what you could possibly want to ask me."

I sat down in the blue arm chair. "Many things. When did you actually meet her?"

"What do you mean, when did I actually meet her?"

"Years ago, at one of Jason Frost's parties?"

"She never came to any of his parties."

"I have a copy of a little movie that proves otherwise."

"What are you talking about?"

"See for yourself."

I set my laptop on the coffee table and showed her the movie. When it was over, she sat silent, twisting her hands in her lap. "Was this party before or after Jason took that picture of the two of you?" I asked.

"I—I don't know," she said. "There were so many parties. I don't remember her being at any of them."

"You look upset. Camden, hold Sherry's hand and help her calm down."

As he reached for her hand, Sherry drew back. "No! I'm all right."

"You're sure?" I asked. "Looks like Diamond was pretty popular. Mitch certainly thought so. So did Tracey."

Sherry's angry glance speared Camden and me. Then she deflated. "After," she said. "It was after he took that picture. I suppose Diamond thought she was part of our group, then. We had a lot of little groupies. She came to a few parties, that's all. Mitch flirted with her. He flirted with everybody."

"Did you have any contact with Diamond before she became your psychic?"

"No." She pushed herself up off the sofa and paced the room. "We posed for the picture. She hung around for a few weeks. You were right. Years later, out of the blue, she called me and offered her services. Our relationship was purely business—from my point of view, anyway—until she quit. Now the police think I killed her. You're still in my employ, aren't you, Randall?"

"You haven't fired me yet."

"Then find out who killed Diamond."

"I didn't think you cared."

"I don't," she said. "I think I'm going to be next."

"Why do you think that?"

She stopped pacing and struck a dramatic pose in front of my chair. "Don't you see? Whoever killed Diamond was trying to get to me through her. Didn't you tell me she wanted me to take her back?"

"Yes, but that was because, as hard as this is for me to believe, she loved you."

Sherry made a dismissive motion. "If she came back, the killer would have someone on the inside."

"Then who do you think this killer is?"

"I don't know! Are you going to help me, or not?"

Since I felt in some way responsible for Diamond's murder, I said, "Yes, I'll help you. Has Patricia called you lately? Has Mitch?

Oh, and speaking of Mitch. Had you planned to buy him out, or was this a spur of the moment decision?"

She sank down on the sofa next to Camden. "Cam, I need peace and quiet. Could we please sit here for a while and let me hold Elise and not talk about any of this?"

"Of course," he said.

She began to sob. "I know I wanted publicity, but not like this."

"People are not going to blame you. Randall will figure it out."

She raised her puffy little eyes to me. "I hope so."

I sat down in the blue arm chair. "When's the last time you saw Mitch Stratton?"

"Years ago."

"When we were talking about him earlier, you said he had changed. Can you be more specific?"

"I'm not sure what that has to do with anything."

"It might be important," I said.

"He was a nice guy, calm and agreeable. But recently, he changed."

"Changed? How?"

"He became aggressive and demanding. He even changed his appearance. I can show you." She took out her phone and scrolled through the pictures.

"You kept his picture?" I asked.

She paused for a moment to give me a glare. "Is there some law that says I can't be sentimental?"

"Excuse me. Carry on."

She found the picture she wanted and showed it to me. Here was Mitch, dressed in a casual blue shirt and jeans, leaning against a bright red Porsche, smiling pleasantly. "Before," she said. She scrolled further down. "After." Gone was the friendly face. Mitch's smile was now tight and shark-like, his body language tense. His suit and tie were dark gray and looked expensive. The dramatic change could be from living with Sherry and her tantrums. It could be from raging jealousy at her success.

It could be the possession and influence of one of those extra evil spirits Lindsey had warned me about.

I showed Camden the pictures. I knew he was thinking the same thing. We'd learned about the evil spirits only a few months ago. Sherry and Mitch had been divorced for at least ten years. But she'd ruined his chances for a career. She'd ruined Crystal Films and now she'd taken over Images. If Mitch's anger had been simmering for that long, it wouldn't take much for a spirit to hop in.

Sherry watched me, frowning. "What are you thinking? You think he had something to do with this? That's impossible!"

"Trust me," I said. "Nothing about any of my cases turns out to be impossible."

# CHAPTER TWENTY-THREE

*"Everybody Dance Now"*

C amden managed to calm Sherry down, and we made sure she was secure in her hotel. Then we headed back to Grace Street. Ellin was home from work and not happy with the latest developments.

"I've just heard Diamond was murdered in her hotel room," she said to Camden. "It's time for you to get out of this."

"When's the last time you saw her?" I asked.

"Yesterday."

"Still on her cell phone?"

"As if it were permanently attached. When I told her to put her phone away, she apologized and got back to work. Cam, I wish you wouldn't get any further involved."

Camden gave her a kiss. "I leave all the rough stuff to Randall."

"Yes, but you're the one who ends up with the black eye."

I had enough time to reheat leftover chicken pie for supper when Kary and her friend came in from a day of job hunting. The friend declined a supper invitation. Camden and Ellin had taken Elise upstairs to continue their conversation, so that left Kary and me at the dining room table with plenty of pie and not much appetite.

"I heard about Diamond," Kary said. "Are you all right?"

"Temporarily," I said. "Everything now points to Sherry's ex-husband, Mitch Stratton, as the culprit. Diamond had those incriminating photos he wanted, and when he couldn't get them, he snapped. I feel somehow responsible for Diamond, but my sensible side tells me Mitch would've killed her anyway. Sherry ruining Images was the last straw. And there's this." I showed her the two pictures of Stratton. "From Hallmark leading man to Best Dressed Demon on *Lucifer*. Guess what zeroed in on all those negative vibes?"

She caught on right away. "One of those evil spirits Lindsey told you about."

"That's what it looks like."

"Well, that adds another layer of concern. Do you have any idea what to do?"

"I have to find him first." I toyed with a bit of pie. "What's the latest on your job search? Did Dellwood have an opening?"

She picked up the serving fork. "Dellwood was a bust."

"Okay. We'll talk about something else."

"Thanks." She scooped out a small piece of pie. "This is delicious. I wish I were really hungry, but it's been a discouraging day."

"Yes, it has."

"If I haven't thanked you enough for the concert ticket, let me thank you again."

"My pleasure. We'll have to go early so Camden can hold Sherry's hand."

Denny sauntered into the kitchen wearing his red kimono and fuzzy slippers. "Good morning, you two! Do I smell chicken pie? David, did you make this?"

"Yes," I said, "and it's six o'clock PM."

"Well, I had to have my beauty sleep. Juggling rehearsals and shows at the Pyramid just about wears me out. How are you, you ravishingly beautiful thing?" he said to Kary. He got a plate from the cabinet and cut a piece of pie. "I hear you have a ticket for tonight's concert. You lucky creature! I wish I could go, but, alas, I'm at the Pyramid. Have to pay the bills, you know. And everyone loves my tribute to Sherry White, so while she's doing her concert, I'll be doing mine."

"We'll be sure to tell you all about it," Kary said. "David, what about Valerie? Are you keeping her in the loop?"

"Sort of. I hope I've steered her away from anything dangerous."

Denny sat down and rearranged the folds of his kimono. "Is that your little groupie?"

"She thinks so."

"David, you are so dashing I'm surprised you don't have scores of young ladies pounding at the windows. Kary would be pushing them off the rooftops."

Kary laughed. "Oh, he'd have to fend for himself."

Denny patted her hand. "That's what I love about you, precious. You always know when I'm teasing."

I paused, a forkful of pie halfway to my mouth. Teasing. "Denny, I think you've solved a mystery for me."

He and Kary stared as I jumped up from the table and ran into my office. With her impish smile and insistence on dancing, hadn't I always thought the little ghost was teasing us? I sent CDs flying as

I hunted for Elliot Adams' rendition of Paul Pratt's "Teasing Rag." I checked the date. 1912. This had to be her song.

In a few minutes I had the CD in the player and grinned as the familiar tune filled the room. Denny and Kary stood at the office door. Denny looked baffled, but Kary was grinning, too.

"Is that it?"

"That's it," I said.

"Heavenly days, what's it?" Denny asked.

"'Teasing Rag,' written in 1912," I said. "With any luck, it's going to set a little spirit free."

\*\*\*

At seven o'clock I drove Kary and Ellin to the auditorium where Sherry graciously chatted with them for a few minutes before she needed to get herself psyched up—literally—for the concert. She and Camden with Elise departed for her dressing room. Then I escorted the ladies to their seats, which were met with approval.

"These are terrific seats," Ellin said.

"Need anything? Drink? Popcorn? She should emote right at you. I told her to look for two beautiful blonds in the third row."

Kary grinned. Ellin made a face.

"Don't you have some body guarding to do, Randall?"

Kary searched her pocketbook. "Ellin, did you bring any tissues? You know we're going to cry, especially if Sherry sings 'Angel of Love.'"

Ellin's search came up with a pack. "I am well prepared."

I told them to enjoy the concert and went to check on the security teams. There was someone stationed at each auditorium door, and one standing outside at each of the two main exits. The exit nearest to the parking lot was guarded by an officer whose nametag read "Hansen."

"Nothing suspicious to report, Randall," he said. "I did see someone matching Stratton's description earlier, but that was you parking your car." He held up the latest equivalent of a walkie talkie. "Did you get one of these?"

Jordan had given me one of the small two way radios. I'd hooked it on my belt. "Right here."

"We're all ready to signal if anyone tries to get in."

Next, I checked on Sherry. She was in her dressing room, Elise in her lap.

"Sherry, we've got someone at every door, so if anyone decides to make a move, we'll be ready."

"I can't believe Mitch has anything to do with this," she said.

"Maybe he doesn't."

*Not good, Dave,* came Elise's voice.

Sherry was tugging at her fluffed out hair, readjusting each curl and didn't notice my startled expression. Was that a warning from Elise? What was the baby trying to tell me?

What do you see? I thought to her, but she just gave me a long stare.

She's too little to understand all the signals, Camden had told me. She's still figuring it out. So "Not good, Dave" could mean anything. But I wasn't going to ignore it.

Can you show me? I asked her.

She started to cry.

"My goodness," Sherry said. "What's the matter, sweetie? Do you miss your daddy? He'll be back soon. He just went to find where mommy is sitting."

Had something happened to her daddy? My mind was working overtime. "Let me hold her," I said.

Sherry handed me the baby and I held her close. "It's okay, Elise." Her cries turned to hiccups, and then she sniffed and stopped.

Finally satisfied with her hair, Sherry leaned forward to apply her lipstick. Then she sat back. "Sometimes I feel as if the whole world is against me. All this business with those photos and Diamond's death—it's so unsettling."

"Go out there and sing," I said. "That'll help."

"Yes, that's what Cam said. You're both right about that."

"Didn't he mellow you out? Where is he?"

"I forgot to autograph the programs for his wife and for Kary. I told him if he'd go get their books, I'd do that before the show." She actually smiled at me. "Kary's a wonderful young woman, Randall. I wish both of you good luck."

"Thanks," I said. "Looks like Elise has calmed down."

She held out her hands. "Come on, Elise. You get to sit with me."

The baby snuggled back into Sherry's arms and closed her eyes. I waited a few moments, but she seemed all right. "Okay, you're all set here," I told Sherry. "See you at intermission."

I stepped out into the hallway and radioed the security team members. Everyone checked in. All clear. I thought I'd play it safe and take another walk around outside.

*Daddy.*

Her voice was anxious. "Lindsey?" I answered. "What's wrong?"

*Be careful outside.*

A warning from Elise *and* from Lindsey? This was beyond unsettling. "What did you see?"

The exit door to the parking lot was the closest. I found Hansen sprawled on the ground. I was reaching for my radio to call for help when I saw something out of the corner of my eye, something I didn't turn around fast enough to avoid. Something went thunk against the back of my neck, and I went down.

\*\*\*

I wasn't sure how long I was out, but somebody had put on hobnail boots and used me for a trampoline. I groaned and tried to roll over, but my hands were tied. I knew from the upholstery smell and the muted roar of the muffler that I was lying on the back seat of the Fury. So who was driving?

I managed to raise my head a few inches. A tall dark-haired man glanced over his shoulder before returning his attention to the road. This was not Hallmark Man. This was pure demon.

"Nice to meet you, Mitch," I said. "Or whoever's walking around in Mitch. Now get out of my car."

"Where are the photos?" he asked. "I know you have them."

"Nope," I said. "They're gone." I tugged at the ropes. There was a little play in them. If I had enough time, I might be able to work free. "Just pull on into the police station. I've got friends there who'll be glad to see you."

"You're lying about the photos. Tell me where they are."

"They have been shredded into confetti," I said. "Now stop the car, get out, and go away. I'll forget this little mishap."

"That's not happening," he said. "And don't think anyone's going to come to the rescue. I've got your radio, and your little pal's in the trunk."

Damn! Camden had seen me in trouble and tried to come to the rescue. What about Elise? Had the concert started? He was coming back to get the baby. Was she in the trunk with him? Or something worse? Why hadn't he used his telekinesis to stop Mitch? My stomach felt full of rocks. "Are you going to tell me your evil plan, or do I have to guess?"

"Thought I'd roll the car off a cliff."

"There aren't any cliffs around here, sorry."

"How about the reservoir, then? I seem to remember one out this way. Can you swim? Probably not with your head kicked in."

Great. I tugged harder at the ropes. I needed something sharp, anything. I couldn't reach my pockets. I searched the cushions, hoping to find a spring sticking out, but I kept the Fury in better condition than that.

"Well, you don't have to tell me your plan because I think I know what happened," I said. "You remembered Diamond from your party days. You might have even suggested she become Sherry's psychic so she could keep you posted about Sherry. You never quite forgave her for ruining your career, did you? She even took your company, renamed it, and made it successful. That must have rankled."

He didn't say anything.

"Then Diamond calls you and says she's left Sherry, and she has some pictures you might like to see. Only she didn't have them, did she? You didn't have to kill her."

"That was an accident," he said, his voice tight. "She wasn't the one I wanted dead."

"Now you're going after Sherry? Are you just going to waltz into the auditorium? Security's better than that."

"That's not going to be a problem. I've got this." He held up my green plastic backstage pass.

Well, hell. That might be a problem. Ow, what was that? My fingers explored the odd object in the crack of the seat. A jagged little piece of chandelier crystal. I rubbed the ropes against it as hard as I could, hoping it was sharp enough to help me. Stratton swung around the curves with unnecessary force. Camden and I were getting jolted like sneakers in a dryer. There was a clunk as my phone fell out of my pocket and slid far from my reach. Well, there went that plan. Finally, I felt the edge of the rope start to fray. I was able to pull one hand free, then the other. Now all I needed was a weapon. Then Stratton swung around the next corner, and Lunch in a Can rolled out from under the seat.

Stratton parked the car, turned to say something gloating, and got a face full of Sunday Picnic. It must not have been very tasty, because he screamed and clawed at his eyes, giving me plenty of time to clonk him on the head with the can and shove him out of the car. I jumped out on top of him and we rolled on the grass. I was pounding him into the ground when I noticed the Fury rolling backward. In our wild scramble out of the car, Stratton's foot must have hit the gear shift.

Stratton had backed into a spot on a slope overlooking the Parkland reservoir. Further up the bank was a popular place for people to come look down at the water rushing into Lower Lake and to toss bread to the carp. No one was allowed this far down because cars might slide into the lake, just as the Fury was about to do.

I'd never run so fast in my life. I reached the car just as the trunk was halfway into the water, swung myself into the driver's seat, and groped for the ignition.

No key.

I yanked the car into park, halting the slide. Ignoring my thundering heartbeat, I searched the floor. Stratton must have dropped it when I attacked. It wasn't on the floor by my feet. It wasn't on the passenger's side floor. To my horror, the Fury gave a groan and slid further back. The bank was giving way.

I ran back to where I'd left Stratton flat out on the ground, but the key wasn't in his pockets. He must have dropped it during our fight. Scrabbling in the grass, my fingers finally closed around the R-shaped key ring Kary had given me for Christmas.

The trunk was almost completely submerged by the time I leaped into the driver's seat. After three tries, the Fury rumbled to life and slowly pulled forward. I kept a steady pressure on the gas, not wanting to lose the car's tenuous grip on the bank. The back tires spun slightly in the mud and then caught in the gravel. Come on, come on. Slowly, the Fury regained the bank and pulled up onto the flat surface of the reservoir. I put the car in park and turned off the ignition, yanked out the key, and got out. On shaky legs, I hurried around and unlocked the trunk. Expecting to see Camden and terrified something had happened to Elise, I stood and gaped as my "little pal" turned out to be Valerie Banner.

She was pale and trembling. "Don't just stand there! Help me out!"

I pulled her from the trunk. "Are you okay? What the hell are you doing in there?"

She pushed me away. "I was trying to help you! I saw this man hit you, and when I tried to fight him off, he shoved me in the trunk. It's Stratton, isn't it?"

From the corner of my eye I saw movement. Before I could warn Valerie, Stratton grabbed her and drew an extremely nasty-looking knife from his belt.

He glared at me. "Give me the key."

Valerie wiggled and tried to stomp on his foot, but he placed the knife at her throat.

"Valerie, be still," I said.

Stratton tightened his grip. "The key, Randall. Now."

Hoping to distract him, I threw the key to one side, but he gave Valerie a push that sent her crashing into me. By the time we'd untangled ourselves he'd jumped into the Fury and roared off.

I helped Valerie to her feet. "Oh, no!" she said. "He's gone after Sherry!" She searched her pockets. "Where's my phone? We have to call and warn her! Call her!"

My phone was somewhere in the back seat of the Fury.

"What are we going to do?" Valerie said. "How are we going to get back to the auditorium?"

Denny's yellow Le Baron screeched to a halt. For one bizarre moment, I thought Sherry had left her concert, stolen Denny's car, and come to the rescue. Then Denny leaned out of the driver's side window, orange wig askew. "Heavenly days, David! Are you okay? Cam called and said you were in dire peril! I rushed from the Pyramid as fast as I could."

I hustled Valerie into the backseat of the Le Baron and jumped in the passenger seat. "Mitch Stratton's after Sherry. Hand me your phone."

Denny passed his cell phone over. "But he won't be able to get in."

"He might," I said. "He has my backstage pass, and we've already been mistaken twice for each other."

"What are you going to do when we get there?" Valerie asked.

I looked at Denny in his Sherry White drag. "I have a plan."

# CHAPTER TWENTY-FOUR

*"Dance Away"*

Jordan let me and Denny in one of the backstage doors. No one matching Stratton's description had tried to get in.

I was never so happy in my life to see Camden and Elise. The baby was asleep.

"She just stopped crying," Camden said. "She was completely in tune with me, so she saw you in danger, and then she saw Denny come to the rescue."

I reached over to cradle her little head in my hand. "I thought the two of you were in the trunk. I couldn't imagine what was going on."

"We're okay," he said.

Even though that was obvious, it made me feel even better to hear him say it. I rubbed the back of my neck. "You sense any Evil Darkness?"

"Not yet."

"Did Stratton admit to murdering Ms. Diamonte?" Jordan asked me.

"He said it was an accident."

"How's Ms. Banner?"

I'd convinced Valerie to sit outside with another officer and be on the lookout for Stratton. She was still pale and a little damp from her trunk adventure, but she was up for the challenge.

"She's okay. I think she got enough excitement for one day."

Jordan glanced at his watch. "It's almost intermission. I'm going to check with my officers."

Sherry came down the hallway to her dressing room. She was pale and a little damp, too, from all her emoting. "I got your message, Randall. Have you seen him? Has he tried anything?"

"No, not a thing" I said. "Don't worry. You wouldn't mind if Denny came in and stood guard for you?"

"That would be excellent," she said. She ran a hand through her rumpled hair. "My hair's a mess."

"I can help you with that," Denny said.

"Even better."

They went inside. Both Camden and Elise had gone very still. "Stratton's here," he said.

"Take Elise into the dressing room," I told him. "I'm ready."

I stood out of sight and waited only a few moments before Stratton walked casually down the hall to Sherry's dressing room and knocked on the door. Sherry stepped out, her back to him, orange curls bouncing.

"Sherry," he said. "It's all over."

"Ooo, watch it, cutie." Denny turned and let Mitch Stratton see his face.

Stratton stopped, shocked, at the sight of Denny in full Sherry White drag, long enough for me to grab him from behind and twist that ugly-looking knife out of his hand.

"She's changed since you saw her last," I said.

"What the hell?" He tried to struggle free, but Denny grabbed him on the other side. "Let go of me! What are you two morons doing?"

"I don't think Sherry wants to see you," I said. "Especially if it's all over."

"Oh, I want to see him, all right!" The real Sherry charged out in extreme diva mode. "I can't believe this! What did you expect to gain? I'm not going to give you one penny!"

I showed her the knife. "He didn't want money."

She gasped and was amazingly speechless for a full minute. Then she revved up to full power. "First Diamond and then me? You crazy bastard!"

She lunged for him, but fortunately Jordan arrived to take charge so Denny and I could hold her back. Ignoring her shrieks, he arrested Stratton for the murder of Angelina Diamonte and for assaulting a police officer.

"Add Valerie and me to those assault charges," I said.

During all this, Sherry continued to rail at Stratton and express her outrage at his betrayal. She didn't stop until Camden put Elise in her arms.

"Sherry," he said. "Please calm down. Let Jordan handle things. You have to sing the second half of your concert."

Elise looked up at her and gurgled happily. Sherry stopped shrieking. After several deep breaths, she handed the baby to Camden, took a big swig of water, tossed her curls, and went back on stage like the pro she was to finish the concert. No one in the audience could've guessed that during intermission she'd almost killed somebody.

\*\*\*

After the concert, I found the Fury double parked behind one of the police cruisers and followed Jordan to the station to give my statement.

"Stratton had been following Sherry for some time, waiting for an opportunity to confront her," I said. "Diamond was his inside resource, and when she found the photos, he was the first one she called. She called Tony Kenner, too. But then she had a change of heart and reneged on both deals. Too bad Diamond wasn't psychic. She could have sensed Stratton would do anything to get his hands on them."

Jordan leaned back in his chair. "So you don't have the photos?"

"I took them to Sherry, and I hope to high heaven she shredded them."

"That bad, huh?"

"A little too risqué for her audience. Her career was slowing down. This would have killed it."

Jordan started to reply when his phone beeped and alarms rang out in the station. I followed him as he sprinted toward the holding cells in the back. Stratton was on the floor of the first cell, two officers bending over him.

"He tried to escape, sir," one said to Jordan. "Ran like a madman against the bars like he was trying to crash through. Hit hard and collapsed."

The other officer nodded, but looked as if he'd seen something else.

Jordan noticed his hesitation. "Anything you'd like to add, Torrance?"

"Sir, you'll think I'm crazy," he said.

"Try me."

"After he hit the bars, I could've sworn I saw this kind of black mist or smoke coming out of him."

"Make sure the EMS team checks for black smoke," Jordan said, heavy on the sarcasm.

Stratton gave a groan and tried to sit up. "Stay down," the first officer warned.

"Where am I?" he said. "What's going on?"

Even though I was almost certain Original Mitch was back, I stepped forward for a closer look at his face. Blood was streaming from his nose and cut lip, and he was understandably confused, but his whole aspect had changed. He looked exactly like the first picture Sherry had showed me, the carefree fellow posed with his red Porsche.

"Jordan," I said, "there are a few things I need to tell you."

\*\*\*

It took a while and a confirming phone call from Camden to explain about the evil spirits. Jordan wasn't completely convinced.

"The 'Devil Made Me Do It' defense doesn't hold up very well in court," he said.

"But we'll see."

I sent Kary a text to let her know I was on my way home. She was waiting for me on the porch and hugged me tight.

"Cam told me what happened," she said. "Are you sure you're all right?"

"Fine," I said. "The spirit's gone, leaving poor old Mitch to face the music. I explained everything as well as I could to Jordan, so we'll hope for the best. How's Sherry? I need to let her know."

Kary tugged on my arm and pulled me toward the door. "Tomorrow's soon enough. It's past your bedtime, mister."

I caught a glimpse of myself before I got into the shower and had to admit I looked pretty ragged after going a round with a possessed Mitch, saving Sherry, and trying to convince Jordan about the serious problem on the Other Side. Once I was clean and dry and safe in my bed with Kary, I went right to sleep and immediately dreamed of Lindsey.

"How many more of those things did you tell me are still out there?" I asked her. "Four maybe?"

*I think so*, she answered. *Good job, Daddy.*

"Can you tell me anything about the next one?"

*No*, she said. *But I'll help you catch it.*

"It's a deal," I said, and my dream ended.

\*\*\*

Sunday morning, everything was so amazingly normal it was hard to believe the events of last night. We had breakfast on the porch, Camden and Elise in the swing, Ellin in the rocking chair next to the swing, and Kary and I in the rocking chairs on either side of the table. There was coffee and iced tea and bagels Ellin had brought home from the bakery on Food Row. Cindy and Oreo sat on the porch railing, tails twitching as cardinals and sparrows continued their on-going battle for seeds at the feeder.

A little drama played out, no doubt the first of many. Elise levitated a leaf. Ellin gave Cam a significant look. He shook his head. Her look intensified. He ignored this and shifted the baby to his other arm. Ellin sighed, took a drink of her coffee, and turned to Kary.

"Anything on your job search?"

"Nothing yet, I'm afraid."

"I'm sure I could find something for you at the PSN," she said, "but I wouldn't be able to pay you what you're worth."

"Thanks," Kary said. "I may have to take you up on that."

Now I got the laser stare. "And how many more of these evil spirits are we going to deal with, Randall?"

"According to Lindsey, four more," I said.

"You need to video your next encounter. I could use a story like this."

"I'll remember that the next time I'm tied up in the back of my car heading for the reservoir." I took another bagel from the dish on the table. "Wish you'd been there, Camden. You could've zapped that black smoke."

"I could've zapped Mitch," he said. "I'm not sure the actual evil spirit is zappable."

"I feel sorry for Mitch," Kary said. "He had this thing inside controlling his actions. He shouldn't have to pay."

"I'll talk to Sherry and see if she'll drop charges," Camden said, "but that still leaves Diamond's murder."

"Which he said was an accident," I said.

A neighbor drove by, and everyone waved. I felt a pang of sadness. I had grown to love Grace Street and all the people who lived here. I didn't know their life histories, like Camden did, but at least I knew their dogs' names and a little something about what was going on. If Kary and I had to move, I would seriously miss this neighborhood.

And I'd miss my responsibilities. Ellin's touch was excellent at erasing Camden's worst visions, but Ellin wasn't always around. And what about Elise? I needed to be here to help her make sense of her own visions and telekinesis, make sure she didn't end up on the front page of the *Galaxy* every week, and definitely make sure she didn't become Princess of the Psychic Service Network.

Before I could get too maudlin, I had a call from Valerie.

"Hey," I said. "Dried out yet?"

Her voice was wildly excited. "Wait till you hear this! I wrote up the story of Stratton's plot to kill Sherry and my escape from certain death, and the *Herald* is going to print it! A real story, David, not some puff piece. Uncle Jake is so proud."

"That's great news," I said. "Congratulations."

"Be sure to tell everyone."

"I will—oh, and Valerie, better say it was an alleged plot."

"Alleged?" she said in disbelief. "But Stratton tried to kill you and me! Both of us!"

I wanted to save the real Mitch, if possible. "Yes, but he wasn't quite himself."

There was a sharp intake of breath. "Do you have inside information?"

"When does your story go to print?" I asked. "We need to talk."

"We have time," she said. "How about this afternoon at Perkie's? Two o'clock?"

"See you there," I said.

\*\*\*

Ellin kept Elise while Camden, Kary, and I went to church. While I have my doubts about there being a heavenly father in the sky, I like to keep my options open, especially when I've just survived a close call. Denny and Lily joined us. They looked splendid in their matching pink sundresses and straw hats trimmed with pink and white ribbons.

Denny was delighted to have played a part in apprehending the killer and saving Sherry, but even more delighted about finding Lily. During the part of the church service when everyone stood to shake hands and wish their fellow members peace, he leaned toward me and whispered, "Who would've thought I'd find my soul mate right next door? God works in mysterious ways, David."

There are indeed mysterious ways, I thought. Not sure God is handing them out.

But Denny and Lily were so happy I wasn't going to say anything to ruin their good fortune. And hadn't I been surprised to find my soul mate when I moved into 302 Grace?

Another reason to stay.

\*\*\*

At two o'clock, I met Valerie at Perkie's Coffee Shop at the park and filled her in on Stratton's behavior. I didn't mention evil spirits. I said I'd uncovered some things in his past that indicated he might be suffering from a mental illness. Valerie took this seriously.

"So there's more to this story," she said.

"If I were you, I'd keep in touch with Jordan Finley at the Parkland PD," I said.

"Thanks, David," she said. "We make a good team."

"Don't start with that again."

She laughed. "Oh, I think I can take it from here."

\*\*\*

On my way home from Perkie's I had a text from Mandy at the library.

"This might help you, David."

Mandy had searched the ancient microfiche and found an article and an old black and white picture from a newspaper celebrating Parkland's history. The article included stories about the older buildings in town: the Parkland Hotel, the original City Hall, and the Parkland Theater. In the picture, I recognized the ballroom, resplendent with sparkling chandeliers and velvety-looking draperies at the long windows. Dozens of couples in turn of the century finery danced, while other guests sat at round tables, watching the dance, eating, and drinking. I enlarged the picture and searched the tiny faces; then read the caption: "The Grand Ball of 1912, formally opened by Mr. Charles Park. Seated with Mr. Park are his wife, Amelia Constance Park, and his daughter, Belle."

Charles Park stood with one arm outstretched as if welcoming the crowd. Amelia Constance, wearing a large fancy hat with curling feathers, stood beside him. Next to her was a young woman, her features blurred by the age and faded quality of the paper, but then, hadn't her features always been indistinct? I'd know the tilt of that head anywhere, the curve of that impish smile.

She was sitting in an ornate wooden wheelchair.

\*\*\*

I wasn't sure anyone would be at the theater Sunday afternoon, but Whitley, the director of *South Pacific*, was in the office and let me in.

"Just doing a little ghost hunting," I explained, and being a theater person, he understood.

"Go on in," he said. "I'll turn on the house lights."

I made my way down the aisle and past the Day-Glo palm trees and polka dotted leaves to the door backstage. The ballroom was empty, but after a few minutes, I heard the soft plaintive notes that introduced "Teasing Rag" and Belle appeared. She came to me, swirling around invitingly. I had to turn to keep her face in view.

"Hello, Belle," I said. "I've got your number now. 1912. And your song, 'Teasing Rag.' That's what you wanted me to find out, wasn't it?"

She smiled, and to my surprise, stopped dancing. She reached up and cupped my face in hands softer than air. For a moment, I thought our lips might meet; then, true to her impish nature, she slipped away, darting across the dark floor like a candle flame. She danced to the edge of the room, turned, blew me a kiss, and vanished.

"She's gone, yes?"

I turned to see the theater custodian Marcos in the doorway.

"Yes," I said. "And I have a feeling she won't be back."

"You discovered why she was here?"

"I had to find her song. It was 'Teasing Rag.'"

"Teasing, eh? So it was a game for her? Now perhaps she will go haunt another ballroom." He chuckled and began to push his long dust mop across the floor. "Just as well. They asked me to clean this for the cast party. Not everyone likes ghosts."

"They're going to party in here? I thought it was going to be torn down."

"There's been a generous donation to the theater to save it. A miracle, no?"

"I'm very glad to hear that," I said. "Who was the donor?"

He shrugged. "It was anonymous. Another mystery for you."

"Believe me," I said. "I've had enough mystery for a long time."

# CHAPTER TWENTY-FIVE

*"Dance Into the Light"*

The following Friday, the cast of *South Pacific* held an opening night party in the ballroom with special guest Sherry White. Not only were they thrilled she could attend, it was revealed that she was the one who had given that generous donation to the Historical Society. The ballroom was saved. The floor had been cleaned and polished until it glistened like a dark lake. There hadn't been time to restore the chandeliers to their former glory, so stage lights beamed soft blues and golds. Music was provided by three members of the show's orchestra who also played regularly at the Pyramid.

I stood toward the back of the ballroom, taking in the scene. Kary, Camden, and Ellin sat at one of the tables arranged along the side of the room while guests and cast members took turns holding Elise. Kary wore a dark blue dress that shimmered in the light, her silky blond hair flowing over her shoulders. Camden was in his gray suit and blue tie, and Ellin looked regal in a dress the color of the red roses that wound around our porch in the summer. Our porch. At our house. This was the family I'd made for myself after the initial heartbreak and sadness of losing Lindsey. I knew I had to be with Kary wherever she was, but leaving 302 Grace Street was going to be one hell of a decision I wasn't prepared to make.

Lily sat with them, elegant in a short black dress and heels, her poofy white hair arranged into a fancy braid. Earlier in the week Denny had packed his matching yellow suitcases and moved in with Lily.

"Now that I have Lily all redecorated, my next challenge is that house," he'd told me.

Denny came up to the microphone. He'd exchanged his costume for a tuxedo, but still wore the Bloody Harry topknot and feathers. He called for attention. "I'd like to thank everyone for a wonderful show tonight, and a special thank you to Sherry White for saving this amazing ballroom." When the cheers and applause died down, he said, "And now I'd like to dedicate this song to my lovely Lily. Not only did she find a perfect Lieutenant Cable for us." He motioned to the actor and paused for another round of applause. "But she embodies everything I feel when Emile sings, 'Once you have found her, never let her go.' My dearest Lily, this is for you."

As Denny sang "Never Let Her Go," I thought of my own feelings for Kary, Camden and Ellin's feelings for each other, and even in some sadly twisted way, Mitch and Sherry's complicated relationship, a relationship that dark spirit had been able to manipulate.

Couples filled the ballroom, dancing slowly to the song. I thought of Belle and the graceful way she had moved around the room, lighter than air. If I closed my eyes, I could see her in the music: glowing, flirting, dancing delightfully in the shadows of the dark empty room. I could see another little girl dancing, too, a little girl with long brown curls and a sweet teasing smile.

*Thank you, Daddy. Thank you for helping Belle. Now she can leave the ballroom. Now she can dance wherever she likes.*

"What are you thinking of, David?"

I opened my eyes. Sherry smiled at me. "You were miles away."

"Just resting."

"I've been talking with Ellin about sponsors," she said. "I'm going to contact Zing Cola and Hairlight Haircare about possibly sponsoring the PSN."

"That would be great."

"I don't think the Christian Girls Alliance would sponsor a psychic show."

"Even if just one of those comes on board, it'll help a lot."

She gave me another smile. "I was glad I could do something. You and Cam saved my life in more than one way, you know. I never realized what an awful person I was. I mean, I was so worried about my career I had to make up that dreadful story to get attention. I'm pretty sure I can be better than that."

"I know you can," I said.

She coiled one orange curl around her finger. "Something else, if you're interested. There's a second grade position open at Parkland Elementary. It's Kary's if she wants it."

As I stared in disbelief, she shrugged.

"What's the use of being famous if you can't push people around?"

"An opening," I said.

"Yes."

"At Parkland Elementary, here in Parkland."

"All she has to do is give them a call."

"Who did you kill?"

She laughed. "One of the teachers decided to take early retirement. I just helped make the deal a little sweeter." She tossed her hair. "Plus she's a fan. Everyone's a fan, Randall. Except you."

Right then, she was the most beautiful woman in the world. I caught her in my arms and gave her a kiss. "First the ballroom, sponsors for Ellin, and now a job for Kary? Tonight, I'm your biggest fan."

She laughed again. "Thank you."

"Did you tell Kary?"

"I thought you'd like to tell her."

"I certainly would."

She touched my arm. "David, I hope this works out for you."

The song finished, and Denny called out, "Sherry, would you honor us with a song?"

"Only if you sing with me," she replied.

"Oh, I wouldn't dare!"

"You're the next best thing to me, aren't you? Of course you'll sing."

As she and Denny belted out an over the top duet of "Angel of Love," I went to ask Kary for this dance and to tell her that 302 Grace Street was still our home.

End

www.ingramcontent.com/pod-product-compliance
Lightning Source LLC
Chambersburg PA
CBHW060914250626
47159CB00008B/3007